NOTES FROM UNDERGROUND
THE HOLLOW EARTH STORY CYCLE

Other books by Orrin Grey

Nonfiction:

Glowing in the Dark: Writings on the Horror Film

Anthologies:

Fungi (with Silvia Moreno-Garcia)

Chapbooks:

Gardinel's Real Estate (with M. S. Corley)
The Mysterious Flame

Collections:

Never Bet the Devil & Other Warnings
Painted Monsters & Other Strange Beasts
Guignol & Other Sardonic Tales
How to See Ghosts & Other Figments

NOTES FROM UNDERGROUND
THE HOLLOW EARTH STORY CYCLE

ORRIN GREY

WORD HORDE
PETALUMA, CA

First Edition

ISBN: 978-1-956252-11-8

A Word Horde Book
www.wordhorde.com

TABLE OF CONTENTS

"The audience knows the truth. The world is simple, miserable, solid all the way through. But if you can fool them, even for a second... then you can make them wonder. And you get to see something very special."
—*The Prestige* (2006)

"It is not worth the while to go round the world to count the cats in Zanzibar. Yet do this till you can do better, and you may perhaps find some 'Symmes' Hole' by which to get at the inside at last."
—Henry David Thoreau, *Walden*

For Edgar Rice Burroughs, Brian McNaughton,
and all the explorers of Hollow Earths
both real and imagined.

PREAMBLE

The book that you hold in your hands—or view on your screen, or hear via your headphones—is different from anything I have ever done before. It is not a novel but nor is it a collection of otherwise-unrelated short stories, of the kind that have occupied my previous volumes such as *How to See Ghosts & Other Figments* or *Painted Monsters & Other Strange Beasts*.

Instead, this is a collection of linked short stories that all share certain elements of setting, of world-building, of *mythos*, for lack of a better word. Not an idea that is unprecedented, certainly, but one which I have never before attempted.

It all started when I got invitations for three different anthologies at the same time. I wanted to contribute stories to all three, but the turnaround times involved and my workload at that moment made doing so…not *impossible*, but certainly difficult. So, I hit upon an idea: I would write three different stories, but all three of them would share similarities of theme and phenomena. Three stories set in what was essentially the same "world."

Like most writers of gothic, weird, and horrific fiction, the world in which the majority of my stories take place—these included—is essentially our own, simply removed, at times, by a step or two. Our workaday world, except that something is true, something we think, sometimes hope isn't true in the world we inhabit. Usually, this truth is an anomaly, even in the story. It is an interruption of the accepted reality of the characters' lives. An irregularity.

It is in this irregularity that most horror stories live and die, and so shaping and deploying that irregularity is of paramount importance to the successful author of horror stories. With the three tales I set out to pen for those three disparate anthologies, I would simply create *one* irregularity, rather than three, and spread it out between them.

These three anthologies covered extremely disparate themes. One was seeking stories taking place on the road ("No Exit"), one called for tales taking place within an asylum or similar institution ("Veteran of the Future Wars"), and one was focused on subterranean horror ("Hollow Earths").

As I worked, however, I realized that I had *already* written an earlier story that also fell into this same "cycle" of linked tales ("The Insectivore"). And once it occurred to me that I had *four* stories in hand, rather than three, the idea of making an entire collection out of this "story cycle" was an obvious one.

From the outset, I knew what the themes of the various stories would be, despite their otherwise disparate natures. Working from those four linked but otherwise largely unrelated stories, I wrote others, for other anthology calls, that filled in areas of the "mythos" that I was building, always with the intent of creating one long novelette, unique to the eventual collection, that would help to center and tie them all together.

Hence, "Leandra's Story" and "Pandora" act as lynchpins to the entire collection, creating a framework for the rest of the stories contained herein, which explore specific nodes within the larger mythology of the Hollow Earth.

**

As for why I chose the Hollow Earth as my thematic building block, I can only say that it is a concept that has always fascinated me. For whatever reason, the idea of a world of unknown explanation that exists beneath our feet—rather than in outer space, or some far-off dimension—resonates with me in a way that no other kind of adventure story ever has.

Nor do I think this book is an exhaustive exploration of my own ideas of the Hollow Earth. If I wrote a new Hollow Earth story tomorrow, it might be something very different indeed.

When I was in high school, I discovered Edgar Rice Burroughs's Pellucidar books in my school library, but even before then I had already been introduced to the idea through comic books and loose cinematic adaptations of Burroughs and Jules Verne. It wasn't until college that I first learned of Hollow Earth theory, and the real explorers, scholars, and weirdos who advanced actual beliefs that the world was filled with fantastical worlds of its own, simply awaiting our exploration.

These individuals (folks like John Cleves

Symmes, Cyrus Teed, and Richard Sharpe Shaver, to name a few), whose theories often combined science, pseudoscience, and religious mysticism, had a huge influence on the shape my own Hollow Earths would eventually take. That their theories were almost inextricably tied to (and sometimes communicated through) early science fiction, weird literature, and the pulps didn't hurt a thing.

In finding my own "Symmes' Hole" to access my particular Hollow Earth and concocting these stories of it, David Standish's 2005 nonfiction book on the history of Hollow Earth theory, simply called *Hollow Earth*, was indispensable. It's also important to mention Mike Mignola's Hellboy and B.P.R.D. comics, with their depictions of a Hollow Earth in decline—inspired by Edward Bulwer-Lytton's 1871 novel *The Coming Race*.

One of my favorite things about the Hollow Earth is that there are usually dinosaurs in it. And yet, there aren't many dinosaurs to be found in these pages. Why is that? I realized as I was writing that my own idea of the Hollow Earth was a place at once physical and metaphysical. A realm as much of dreams as of earth, where time existed differently, and where even eternity could come to an end.

The Utopian visions of the Hollow Earth which so appealed to the writers, the dreamers, and the outcasts of the 19th century no longer felt apropos for my stories, and so that once golden realm deteriorated into something more sinister—or seemingly so. To say much more would perhaps give away too much.

Yet, there's a bit more to add. All the stories in this volume are not directly concerned with the Hollow Earth. Other threads interweave, to paint a picture of the past, the present, and the future. Some draw their inspiration not directly from the stories of the world beneath our feet, but of worlds yet to come—specifically, a relatively throwaway line in H. P. Lovecraft's *The Shadow Out of Time*: "After man there would be the mighty beetle civilization, the bodies of whose members the cream of the Great Race would seize when the monstrous doom overtook the elder world."

These future coleopteran inhabitants who replace humanity following climatic disaster also make their way into these stories, and the two threads interweave, as the beetles clash with the inhabitants of the inner earth. And there are other elements, too. Intermediary steps between humans and these beetles, as described in "New, and Strangely Bodied."

Because the Hollow Earth, as I envision it, is a sea which touches all of these shores, all of them can interact in the same book—sometimes within the same story. The result was a strange and heady treat to write, sampling from a wide array of extremely disparate influences to create a concoction that is, I hope, also a pleasure to imbibe.

THE INSECTIVORE

There was an old man on our street who ate bugs. Beetles, pill bugs, those things that my mom called locusts that were actually cicadas. Anything with a crunchy exoskeleton, pretty much.

We'd see him sometimes, picking cicadas off the trees, hanging out under the street-lights at night, scooping up June bugs. On the porch of his house were a dozen of those bug zappers, with their eerie purple-blue glow and their low-key buzzing. They were a buffet line to him. Us kids would stand on the other side of the street and watch as he walked from one to the next, picking out the beetles be-tween two fingers and popping them into his mouth—a delicacy!

His name was Mr. Petrie, and he lived all alone in an old two-story house that had once been white but was now fading to gray. Its windows always looked dark, and the porch was screened with trellises, though nothing grew on them but the occasional brown vine. As kids, he was a figure of equal parts fascination and terror to us, and we'd sometimes dare each other to go up and peer in those darkened windows, but we rarely saw much when we did. Old furniture, dirty dishes. Desks and sideboards stacked deep with books and papers and objects that were indiscernible in the gloom.

Of the old man himself we saw plenty. Though he wasn't exactly social, he came out of his house all the time to wander the streets looking for bugs to eat. He seemed pretty unassuming, old and bald with papery skin over his skull, always wearing old-fashioned brown suits that I imagined smelled like mothballs, though when I was little I never got close enough to find out.

I was born early enough and our town was small enough that the paranoia concerning the safety of young children that seems to define our age hadn't yet taken hold, and the parents on our street considered him harmless, "just a crazy old man."

He lived off Social Security or a pension or

something, so he didn't have to go to work. He just walked around the streets talking to himself and eating bugs. Sometimes I'd see him hanging around in front of the library or the post office. Sometimes I saw him coming home carrying armfuls of books. He got groceries delivered to him from the Golden Apple Grocery—an older boy with shaggy blond hair pulled up in a hatchback car and unloaded brown paper bags up to the front door of that old, dark house.

When I was a little older, I was that boy. I had a job behind the video counter at the Golden Apple and, because I had my dad's old Subaru and a driver's license, I got the task of doing the deliveries, hauling bags of groceries to old ladies and the guy who'd lost his leg in Vietnam and other people who couldn't come get them on their own.

How exactly Mr. Petrie made that list I couldn't say, since he seemed to still be able to get around just fine, but maybe mental stability was factored in. Anyway, that's how I got to get closer to Mr. Petrie's house—and Mr. Petrie himself—than any of us ever had as kids, and why I got a ringside seat to what ultimately became of him.

***

The first time I delivered groceries to Mr. Petrie, I was still pretty scared of him. The house seemed a little smaller now that I was in high school, but it was no less dark, the faded paint no less peeling, the whole edifice no less grim. The first time I walked up his creaking front steps and pushed the button on the doorbell, my skin crawled.

On the other side of the door I heard a sound, a rustling, like something big moving under a bunch of newspaper. I imagined a giant cockroach, scuttling out from under the refuse that cluttered the house and creeping toward the door. I imagined the door opening inward onto darkness, and rough, segmented legs reaching out to draw me in. I wanted to run, but I knew that Mr. Jorgen at the Golden Apple was expecting me to come back with payment, so I couldn't.

I don't know why I pictured Mr. Petrie as a giant cockroach—I hadn't yet read "The Metamorphosis," and wouldn't until college. You are what you eat, maybe? That's what my mind's eye conjured, anyway, and when I heard something on the other side of the door, and then saw the door begin to fall open, the bags slipped out of my hands and split on the porch, spilling onions and a single orange to go rolling across the uneven boards.

That distracted me, and when I looked back up, there was Mr. Petrie, looking as he had when I was a little kid. Not a monstrous insect, just an old man in a rumpled brown suit. He blinked at me, and at the groceries that lay scattered on the porch, and I began stammering an apology, and offering to help him gather them up, to carry them inside. And that's how I wound up stepping into Mr. Petrie's house for the first time.

Given his dietary predilections, imagining Mr. Petrie as a giant spider, rather than a cockroach, would probably have been more apt, but it didn't occur to me until I was already stepping across his threshold. At that moment, the whole "welcome to my parlor" thing popped into my head, and I called up images of Mr. Petrie standing behind me, his shadow crawling up the wall, sprouting too many arms. But still, as I glanced back, he was just an unassuming, sad-looking old man. Nothing terribly sinister.

His house was dark inside, even in daylight. When I went back out to my car and looked back up at the house, I realized it was because all the windows were strangely recessed, sinking them in wells of shadow. From inside the house, it just looked like the sun was always shining the wrong way, always turning a corner to avoid coming inside.

It wasn't as dark in the house as I'd always imagined when I was a kid, though. There were lamps with dusty shades standing here and there, casting little spheres of light that I'd struggle to call golden but also wouldn't quite just call yellow. From inside, the whole house looked like an antique store or a museum that someone had long since abandoned to neglect. Cobwebs were everywhere except in the main thoroughfares, and all the furniture seemed to be piled with discarded papers and other bric-a-brac.

Then there were the bugs. Wherever I looked there were glass cases filled with insects pinned to boards. Not just beetles, either. The walls were hung with butterflies and moths preserved behind two sheets of glass, their wings still iridescent even in the dull light. Insect collections like the ones you see in the 4H building at the state fair lay on desks and chairs, some of them completely enclosed in glass cases and bearing careful hand-lettered labels, others open to the air in various stages of dissolution or deconstruction. There were bell jars and mason jars, and just about everything made of glass in the place seemed to hold at least one dead bug.

I saw everything out of the corner of my eye, just jumbled impressions of the mosaicked shadow-space that was the interior of Mr. Petrie's house as I carried groceries in handfuls into the kitchen at the back. I don't really know what I expected to find there—ice cube trays piled full of pill bugs, meals left out to rot—but aside from the same signs of neglect that were everywhere in the house, the kitchen looked no different than any other kitchen I had ever seen.

As Mr. Petrie was walking me back to the front door and pressing some crumpled bills into my hand in payment for the groceries, it struck me for the first time in all my then-seventeen years that Mr. Petrie must have once had a family. As kids we'd sometimes seen an adult son come to visit, parking a silver car along the side of the road and going up to ring the bell on the front door. He didn't come often, and never stayed long,

and if Mr. Petrie had any grandchildren, he
never brought them by. But once Mr. Petrie
must have had a wife, and she and the son
must have lived in this house with him, and
I realized as I walked back to my car that the
house was less the home of a madman than
an archaeological relic, the ruins of a life that
had crumbled under some unguessed weight.

After that, I brought all of Mr. Petrie's groceries through to the kitchen, though I gathered
that I was the first delivery boy to ever do so.
Soon, I wasn't even coming up to the front
door at all, but walking around the house to
the screened-in back porch where Mr. Petrie
often sat. Over time, he came to tolerate me
pretty well, if not exactly *like* me, or maybe
he was just lonely. Whatever the case, he began to open up to me, and so I learned his
odd story, or some of it.

Mr. Petrie had been a psychic. Not just ca-
sually, he did it for a living. He didn't start
out that way. First he was an eighth grade
social studies teacher, but he started doing
psychic readings on the side, and eventually
it became his career. He toured the country,
gave lectures, went on the radio and the TV,

wrote two books. That last part, at least, was true, because I saw them.

So what happened? "I was a fraud," he told me. "Oh, not on purpose. I really believed in what I was doing. But at best I was squandering my gift, using it for frivolous things. 'Is my husband seeing another woman? Where did Aunt Ida leave her jewelry?' There wasn't much call for finding bodies or tracking down killers, like you see on TV. It turns out that psychics go over badly in the courtroom. But I had no complaints, until I experienced a *real* vision."

Apparently, this real psychic vision didn't happen all at once. It came to him piecemeal, a bit at a time, over the course of months. When it did finally come together, though, it ruined him, destroyed his life. It concerned the fate of the world after humanity had died out, and the race of coleopteran people who would ultimately take our place. Not kill us off, he was unclear about what did that, just rise to fill our niche. I had to ask him what "coleopteran" meant, and he replied, "Beetles, son. We're going to be replaced by beetles."

So, there was the root of his odd mania, anyway, at least according to him. At first, he'd gone about it in different ways. He'd tried to warn people, to take the audience that his psychic abilities had gained him and tell them about what was coming, maybe try to prevent it. To change the course of humanity so that we would never die out, so that *they* would never evolve.

Since he didn't know what destroyed us, he focused on what he *did* know: the identity of our successors. He'd gone to the civil authorities, tried to go on TV, but no one listened. "People don't want a genuine psychic revelation," he said. "They want comforting parlor games, the sense that there are invisible threads that hold the world together. They don't want to know that the world is vast and grim and hungry. They know that already."

As he became increasingly obsessed with this glimpse of the future, it gradually destroyed his marriage and his relationship with his children—I learned that, in addition to the son, he also had a grown daughter, who never spoke to him at all anymore—just as it destroyed his credibility and his career. "Ironic," he said, "the one time I can be really sure I saw something was the one time no one would listen."

None of this fully explained his odd dietary habits, however, and it took months of talking with him, bringing him his groceries and sitting with him on the screened-in back porch where June bugs sometimes caught their hooked feet in the wire, before he finally explained it in any way that made even a little sense.

"There's a story by Ray Bradbury, maybe you read it in school—"

"We read *Fahrenheit 451*."

He ignored me. "It's about these people who arrange time travel safaris—to hunt dinosaurs and things, you know? Anyway, they're very careful. They have these floating paths they walk on, and they only kill things that are about to die anyway, so that they don't do anything to change the future. But one time a guy falls off the path, and he kills a butterfly, I think. And then when he goes back to the future, he finds that the world is a completely different place, just because he killed that one butterfly. Do you understand?"

I told him I didn't, but he didn't really seem to hear me. "The thing is," he said, "I think they know that I know. The beetle people. I mean, they must have history books, right, something that tells them about what came before? Beetle archaeologists digging up fossils of man's reign on earth, just as we dig up the dinosaurs. I think they know that I'm onto them, and I think that one of these days one of them will come back in time to kill me, to put a stop to me before I can put a stop to them. I tried warning people, tried stopping them through organized force, but maybe I don't have to. Maybe if I just find that one right butterfly…"

I continued taking Mr. Petrie his groceries until I left for college. The summer after my freshman year, I came back home and moved back into my upstairs room, which remained unchanged from how I'd left it, except that my mom had moved her sewing machine in there to get more light. I got another job at the Golden Apple Grocery, though someone new was standing behind the video counter looking bored and helping old ladies reach movies off the top shelf, so I ended up unloading trucks as they came in.

There was a new kid doing the deliveries—he drove a pickup, and had hair that fell down over his eyes. I asked the manager about Mr. Petrie, and he said that after I left the old man stopped taking his deliveries the old way. He still phoned in the orders every week, but now he mailed a check, and the delivery kid just left his bags on the front porch.

After I'd been back home for three weeks, I tried going to see Mr. Petrie. For old time's sake, I guess, or maybe because I was curious, or because I felt sorry for him. Distance from my childhood and from the town had taught me that Mr. Petrie was probably schizophrenic or something, probably in need of better care than he had ever gotten.

When I approached the house, it was as dark as ever, the paint now completely faded to gray and flaking off in swaths. The lawn needed mowing. Back when I was a kid Mr. Petrie had always mowed it with an ancient push-mower, and once I started taking his groceries to him I would bring our newer mower up and cut the grass once every couple of weeks. It didn't look like anyone had gotten to it since I'd been gone, and I felt a stab of guilt at going away without giving the old man a second thought. There were dandelions sprouting everywhere, growing almost obscenely long, their heads weighted down with seeds. Other than that the house looked just as I remembered it, except that the bug zappers were gone from the porch.

I rang the bell and peered in, but could see nothing through the gloom inside. There didn't seem to be any lights on beyond the windows that I could see, and while I occasionally thought I detected movement in the dimness, I could never be sure.

I walked around to the screened-in back porch. The back yard was in even worse repair than the front. Grass grew up past my knees, and an old birdbath just barely poked above the verge, with only a bit of brown water standing in the center of it. The porch was empty, the metal chairs on which Mr. Petrie normally sat just crouching there in the gloom. The back door was locked, which I knew could only be accomplished with a hook-and-eye on the inside. So if Mr. Petrie wasn't home, he must have gone out the front.

I went by a couple more times over the next few weeks, and the thought occurred to me that maybe Mr. Petrie had died while I was away—he must have been getting on in years, since he had been an old man in my memory for as long as I had been alive. I wondered how I would know if he had. Who would I ask? Aside from me, who in town really knew him? I asked Mr. Jorgen at the Golden Apple and he told me that the phone calls still came in every week, regular as clockwork, but when I asked my mom when the last time she'd seen Mr. Petrie was, she couldn't recall.

If not for that mystery, I might not have been paying close enough attention to see what happened next. I had my own life now, after all, my own concerns. I'd met a girl in my freshman ethics class—with straight brown hair down her back, and cute freckles across her shoulders and cheeks—and I spent a lot of time on the phone with her that summer, since she'd gone back home too, a couple of states away. But Mr. Petrie's absence made me wonder, and wondering made me watchful. I could see just a corner of his house out of my bedroom window, and at night, when I was waiting to go to sleep, my arms sore from unloading boxes, I would look out that window at the dark shape of his house past the streetlights.

That's why I saw it, a flash of purple-blue light, like one of Mr. Petrie's bug zappers

going off. But they were gone, all of them
missing from their hooks on the porch, and
the flash had seemed too bright for that anyway. It was enough to drag me out of my
bed—where sleep was hard in coming, the
summer night sticky, my parents, as always,
too cheap to run the window units after dark.

I pulled on my shoes and crept downstairs,
not turning on any lights, not waking anyone, and out the door and onto the street. I
passed under the streetlights and beneath the
trees where, as a kid, I had seen Mr. Petrie
eating bugs. I went up the front steps of his
darkened house, but not onto the porch.

I don't know what made me hesitate. Why
I didn't just ring the doorbell—besides that it
was two in the morning—and instead slipped
around the side of the house. I felt like a kid
again, that thrill up your spine that comes
with trespassing, with transgressing. I felt like
I was on a dare, creeping up to peer into Mr.
Petrie's darkened windows.

There was a glow coming from the back of
the house, and my first thought was that Mr.
Petrie had moved all his bug zappers to the
screened-in back porch, though what good
they were going to do back there I couldn't

say. But no, the glow wasn't coming from bug zappers. It was brighter, and it emanated from a single source.

In that unearthly light, I saw Mr. Petrie. He knelt on the all-weather carpet next to his favorite chair, his hands held up in some kind of supplication, his mouth moving constantly, though I couldn't hear any words coming out. He looked like he'd aged ten years in the few months it had been since I saw him last, the strange violet light mottling his complexion, making his already papery skin look almost translucent.

Before him stood what I initially took to be a man in a suit of armor, but there was something wrong about that. The shape was a little off, the plates too shiny. The glow was coming from this figure, somehow. Radiating from it like a cave fungus, oozing out from beneath the plates of its armor, from the gap between the horns that sprouted from its head. Below the arms, two smaller, supplementary arms jutted, and between them they held a ball of squirming purple-blue light. We'd learned about plasma in my freshman science class— the boiling, liquid energy of which the sun is made—and aside from the color, this was exactly how I'd pictured it.

It was the arms that made the figure make sense—the horns sprouting from the helmet not horns at all but antennae, working gently back and forth, the glowing orifice below a nest of moving mouth-parts, the armor a carapace from which lace-delicate wings might unfurl.

In that final moment, I think Mr. Petrie saw me. He looked over, his eyes black in the strange light, and he seemed like he was about to speak to me, but then the ball of energy that the armored figure held leapt from its hands, arced through the space of the porch and touched Mr. Petrie. For a moment he was made translucent by the light, his skeleton visible through his parchment flesh, and then the whole scene exploded in a flash that left miniature purple suns dancing in my vision.

Neighbors reported seeing a bright light in the back of Mr. Petrie's house, and when the sheriff broke in they found nothing of Mr. Petrie or the thing that had killed him except a singed spot on the carpet and a pile of black ash. Chalk another one up to those reports of unexplainable spontaneous human combustion. I looked it up later, and found that there have been over 200 unverified reports over the years. That's something to think about, late at night.

I was gone before the sheriff arrived, and no one ever reported seeing me near the house. No one asked me about what had happened, and I never told. Mr. Petrie's own life lessons had taught me the reward that came with sharing that kind of revelation.

Here's what I wonder, though: If old Mr. Petrie really was some kind of real-deal psychic, could he have conjured up the specter of his own demise from nothing more than his own fear? Would he have had the power to create the thing that he believed was one day going to kill him, a kind of psychic suicide? And do I find that thought more or less distressing than a beetle assassin come back from the future to slay him with a lightning bolt?

NEW, AND STRANGELY BODIED

The first of the bodies that washed up on the beach crawled three feet before it stopped and lay still. Sheriff Perkins said that it was the tide, pushing the body around, but I was there with my camera, and the tide was way out, never came up that far at all, and there were little round holes in the sand, all in a curving line, where fingertips had dug in and pulled it along.

The body itself reminded me of movies I had seen in the past—the special effects that are supposed to be bad, unrealistic, not what a body actually looks like. The Claymation transformations at the end of *Evil Dead*; what a film school friend once called "a lamb chop with an eyeball stapled on it" in Fulci films.

It didn't really look like anything that had once been human, except for the bones. It looked like something made out of the sea, and the things that live in the sea. Anemones, jellyfish, corals, seaweed. All built around the framework of a human skeleton, one arm outstretched, calcified fingers digging into the sand.

Next morning's paper confirmed the former humanity of the corpse with the headline, "Body Found Near Hodgson Cove." One of my photos was underneath. Not of the body, just the sheriff's cruiser parked in the sand, red and blue lights washed to grayscale because the Bridgeport paper wasn't big enough to print in color. The article itself was mostly day one journalism stuff: who, what, when, where, but not any why. The reporter had asked the coroner about cause of death, at least, and had gotten the noncommittal response, "Seems like it's been down there a long time."

When the second body washed up, I was sound asleep in the back room of Cargo Cult Video. The Cargo Cult had a couple of back rooms, connected to the store by a long, narrow hallway paneled in fake wood. One was used for storage, and the other was where I lived.

It looked a lot like it had when it had been

Rob's instead of mine—an old futon in the corner piled with random blankets, a TV stacked on top of an old entertainment center and hooked to a couple of different VCRs and DVD players. I hadn't added much in the way of feminine touches; I wasn't really a feminine touches kind of girl. There was a bathroom with a stand-up-only shower, and for food I used the kitchenette and the fridge in what had been the employee break room, back when the Cult had any such thing as employees.

The phone was on the wall in the hallway, one of those yellowy plastic jobs with a long corkscrew cord. I had put in a cordless phone up front that rang a different number, so I could switch it to voicemail when the store was closed.

While the back room was mostly dark, the blinds let in light from the alley that ran between the back of the store and a wooded gully where water from the hills drained down into the bay. I stumbled out of bed and knocked the phone off the wall before fumbling around in the dark to pick it up. "How soon can you get down to Hodgson Cove?" a familiar voice asked from the other end.

"They found another one."

I had a friend at the coroner's office, Rudy.
He told me that the bodies were filled with
things that he had never seen before. Not really bodies at all; just skeletons, eaten away
by fish and other sea creatures, all the cracks
and crevices, all the chambers and compart-
ments filled up now with slugs and jellies and
anemones and corals. Strange living things
caught halfway between plant and animal,
all of them thriving inside these corpses. "Almost like they're trying to find some sort of
equilibrium," he said. "A symbiosis. To make
something more than the sum of their parts."

Rudy was a smart kid, working at the coroner's office during the summer to help pay
his way through med school down the coast
the rest of the year, but he also read a lot of
science fiction magazines. I'd met him when
he came down to the Cargo Cult, where he
always wanted the weirdest foreign stuff I
could rent him. Pornographic anime, cheapie
college movies about alien abductions or de-
mons that knew kung fu.

The official story that the sheriff's office
eventually came up with involved the *Seagrass*. It had gone down off the coast a couple

of months ago, with all hands on board. A big blow had come up unexpectedly and turned the fishing trawler over in the water, sending her straight down to the bottom. The bodies had never been recovered, and they'd lain down there, trapped in the wreckage, where they'd undergone a sea change into something rich and strange. Now, a deep-sea current was carrying them up to the shore, one by one, and the transformations that time and tide had wreaked on them were just the result of their being down so long.

Of course, that didn't do much to explain why each one was making it farther and farther inland. After the third body was found on the side of the coastal highway, its mushy fingertips like gelatin on the edge of the asphalt, I had a dream.

Like a lot of my dreams, it started with me at work. I was closing down the Cargo Cult for the night, shutting off the neon signs and the lights, checking the back porno room to make sure that no extra perverts were stowing away back there, when I saw someone standing outside the front door.

They were little more than a shadow in the dark, a silhouette against the light of the streetlamp. Even so, they looked somehow wrong. As though they tapered from the bottom to the top, like someone dressed in ecclesiastical robes. "We're closed," I shouted from where I stood, but the shadow didn't budge.

There was a gun in the back room, under the bed, that I had fired maybe three times in my life—another bequest from Rob—and I kept an old, scarred-up baseball bat leaning behind the counter, just in case, but I didn't move toward either of them. Instead, I walked to the front door.

The door was glass from top to bottom, and the figure stood just off our front step, on the old boardwalk, giving me an unobstructed view, had I switched the porch light back on. Something made me stop, though, and instead I opted to flick on the neon OPEN sign, painting the porch in reds and blues that made a purple light.

When I did so, I expected to see one of the crew of the *Seagrass*, a nautical zombie with its face eaten away and wriggling with worms or the fronds of anemones. Instead, it was someone I almost recognized. Dressed, as I had thought, in the robes of the clergy. Starfish clung to his vestments, fish swam around him in the night air, and an octopus wound its thin tendrils about his feet.

In his hands he held a bell, and on it was carved a face at once humanoid and monstrous, its mouth an open circle, its eyes filled with wrath. Its beard was made of sea foam, its crown a bed of coral. The figure rang the bell, and I heard it echo from somewhere out over the water, or out under it. Ding-dong, bell.

While I wasn't sure what the dream meant when I woke up, I remembered where I knew the figure from. It had reminded me of old archival photos that I had seen at the newspaper office, and it had also reminded me of Rob, even though the two looked nothing alike.

What is there to tell about Rob? He was in the army for a while, but he never deployed overseas. He was driving a Jeep on a base someplace down in Oklahoma, and there was a head-on collision. The guy driving the other truck had been drinking. Everybody walked away, except for Rob.

His seatbelt, of all things, cut him almost completely in two; paralyzed him from the waist down. "Can't feel a fucking thing down there," he'd say, demonstrating by poking himself in the thigh with a pen or a letter opener or whatever pointy object he happened to have on hand. "Not even a twitch. Doesn't mean I don't still suck a mean cock, though, when the opportunity presents itself."

And that was Rob. He used the disability pension that he got from the army to open up the Cargo Cult Video store in Bridgeport, and live out of the rooms in the back. The store was the only rental place in town, besides a few mainstream movies in a corner of the local Golden Apple Grocery and a spinner rack at the Rapid Stop on the corner of Langdon and Market.

But rentals weren't the Cult's main source of revenue, not even in those early days. Rob sold videos through the mail—VHS back then, DVDs later—of stuff that was hard to find, stuff that he had to order from overseas or drive down to LA or other, more distant places to pick up.

Cargo Cult carried things like *Traces of Death* and Stanislaw Gauvin's *Demogorgon* and *Tribesmen*, the movie where the cast and crew famously went crazy on some island and actually filmed killing each other. The back storeroom was where Rob kept movies that were too outré for the regular clientele, or that he was preparing to ship.

That was all before I knew him. Rob gave me my first job when I was fresh out of film school down in Eugene, back when I still thought I was going to head down the coast to La La Land and become a DOP.

I worked on a couple of no-budget local horror flicks with guys that I knew from film school; all guerilla filmmaking, *Evil Dead*-style. I remember one special effects guy who had come up with this sort of stop-motion way to make the corpses decompose using sculpey and melting wax, with these bright, almost phosphorescent fungi sprouting up from the bodies. I helped him figure out how to get the timing of the exposures right to make the process work. "When you think about it," he said once, "rotting isn't really going away, like we think it is. It's just getting a new body."

Later, I would think about that in relation to my own mom, embalmed and lying in the ground back in Phoenix, and Rob, who had

been cremated, as per his wishes, his ashes
scattered in the bay, so there was probably no
new body for him. Which maybe that would
be the way he wanted it; he'd never been that
fond of his old body, anyway. "Too short, too
fat, too hairy," he'd say. "It's a good thing I'm
a sex machine, or I'd never get any action at
all."

Back then, I was just a chubby girl leaning toward goth with nothing but a camera
that seemed expensive as hell at the time and
would be shitty now, and a lot of big dreams
that never happened. Rob gave me a job
working the counter at the Cargo Cult while
he prepared movies to ship out in the back
room, or traveled around to pick up more
stock. It was just the two of us, and back then
he was pretty much the only friend I really
had. He always told me I was going on to bigger and better things, and I always wondered
how he could believe in anything, given what
had happened to him.

"What happened?" he asked me one night
when we were closing up and I made the faux
pas of saying something about it. "I had something shitty happen to me. Who hasn't? And
in return I got something great. I fucking love

this place," he said, gesturing around at the Cargo Cult, with its low ceilings and musty carpeting and dim rows of weird-ass movies. "What do I have to be unhappy about?"

In those days I thought I had a lot to be unhappy about. I hated my figure and while I had finally come out as a lesbian while I was in film school, there wasn't exactly a big dating pool in Bridgeport, even if I had been hotter. Now, I dunno... I think maybe trying so hard to be happy is what makes everybody so damned unhappy.

Even while I thought of myself as pretty pissed off, I liked working at the Cult, and I liked Rob. We screened all kinds of crazy shit up on the monitors in the store, not too concerned with what the folks who came in might think. I remember watching *Hausu* and wondering if Rob had slipped me some mushrooms without telling me.

It took me six years of standing behind that counter, popping bubblegum at the customers and watching weird-ass movies before I realized that I was never going to California, was never going to be behind the camera of anything with a budget that you couldn't scrape together with a stay at one of those

clinical research trials. So, I quit the Cult
and went back to school, this time majoring
in photography. I got pretty good at it, and
found that I liked shooting still photos better
than I had ever liked working in the movies.

I don't know what would have happened
then, if things had gone different, but the
week after I received my diploma I got word
that my mom had died back in Phoenix. I
flew down there for two weeks to settle up
her shit, and by the time I got back home I
heard that Rob was gone, too. Complications
from some surgery. I hadn't talked to him in
a couple of years, had just fucking abandoned
him when I went back to school, didn't even
call, and yet he had left the store to me, the
whole business, and the building, which he
apparently owned outright.

Of course, right before graduation, I had
also broken up with Lynne. Not knowing
what else to do with myself, I drove back to
Bridgeport with everything I owned piled
in what had been my mom's station wagon.
With nowhere else to go, I moved into Rob's
old rooms at the back of the Cargo Cult. I
think that I expected to just clean the place
up and get it sold, but it didn't work that way,

and four years later, I still lived there, in those same back rooms, running that same weird video store, though by then our selection was a lot more DVDs than VHS tapes.

Back in the old days, Rob used to put out this catalog. Black-and-white pages on newsprint with grainy photos of video covers and creased posters, and two-or-three-sentence descriptions of the movies, the more lurid the better. That's how he found customers in the days before the Internet. Now, I sold almost everything online, through a catalog on the poorly-pieced-together Cargo Cult website, and through listings on places like eBay.

Rob's disability pension had always been what allowed Cargo Cult to stay afloat, though, and I didn't have that, so I supplemented my income by taking pictures for the *Bridgeport Journal Gazette*, a local newspaper that seemed like it had gotten its name by pulling a handful of options out of a particularly large hat.

They didn't ever put me on the payroll—they only had one full-time photographer, a girl in her twenties who had mostly taken wedding photos before landing this gig and always did the puff pictures of store openings and city council meetings. Instead, I got free-lancer pay to take the occasional more news-worthy story that required me to drag my ass out of bed at three in the morning, or close the store down unexpectedly for forty min-utes while I drove to the other side of town for pictures of a fender bender along the coast highway.

After my weird dream, I was pretty sure that the bodies we had been finding didn't have anything to do with the wrecked *Seagrass*. I didn't open up the Cult that day, and instead drove around to the offices of the *Journal Ga-zette*, which occupied one floor of a narrow, three-story stone building across the street from the wharf, where I dug through the ar-chives until I found what the dream had re-minded me of.

Up on top of the cliff, near where the bridge that gave the town its name crossed the bay, there was an old clapboard church. It stood back off the road now, a rutted gravel path grown up with weeds the only way to get even a Jeep up to it.

I'd never been up there myself, but it was the genius loci of a lot of urban legends around town. Word had it that the church had originally been some stripe of Baptist, and that another kind of preacher had taken up residence there when the Baptists cleared out. A cult leader who called himself Obediah Blum, he preached that a new race of man was coming to replace humanity, whose time was rapidly drawing to a close.

"They will come up from the sea," he'd said. "And they will be like men, but new and strangely bodied. And though we will not know them at first, they will be our successors, and it will be for them to inherit the earth that we leave behind."

The story went that he re-christened the church to Neptune and Poseidon, named it the Esoteric Order, without any further preamble or clarification, and attracted quite a little following before the locals got tired of him. A lynching party came one night in the middle of one of Blum's sermons, dragged him out of his church in front of his whole congregation, and hanged him from the bridge. Local ghost stories said that he could still be seen dangling there on some foggy nights, though now his body was encrusted with barnacles and grown through with coral.

Another version said that a giant hand—or maybe it was a tentacle, or the claw of some huge crab—had reached up and plucked Blum's body from the bridge, dragging it down into the briny depths.

After that, Blum's entire congregation went and drowned themselves. Just walked out into the ocean with stones in their pockets. Nothing about any of this was contained directly in the archives of the *Bridgeport Journal Gazette*—the paper didn't go back that far, having been founded back in '82—just references to it in other stories. These events weren't exactly ancient history in Bridgeport, though. Not something from before Oregon was a state, like some of the tall tales that floated around up and down the coast. This had happened just a few years ago, in the early seventies, when everyone was still afraid of the next Charlie Manson. There were still people around who could remember it.

Blum was who I had recognized in my dream, his round, bald face immortalized in some blurry black-and-white archival photo. The *Bridgeport Journal Gazette* didn't have whatever I was after, though, so I got into my Range Rover—which had replaced Mom's old station wagon a few years back—and drove across the bridge and up to the rutted track that led to the old church, the weeds brushing the underside of the chassis.

I'm not sure exactly what I went up there looking for. The *Gazette* wasn't running my pictures of the bodies themselves—too graphic, my editor told me—but I thought maybe if I could tie them into the old story about Blum and his cult, I could sell them somewhere else; a bigger magazine, or at least some kind of *Fortean Times* or *Weekly World News* sort of operation.

The church wasn't immediately visible from the main road, and even once it was, coming out from behind the trees as the track took a slight bend, it just looked like any other church. White clapboards turned gray by time and the wind from the ocean, a steeple that stood up above the front door. The only difference was the sign out front, hand painted, that said "Esoteric Order" above a symbol that looked a little bit like those Jesus fish that some people had plastered on the backs of their cars, though also somehow different in a way that I couldn't pin down.

I parked and walked up to the front of the

church. Graffiti marred the front door, everything from "Jack Loves Miranda" to "Blum
had it right" to pentagrams and drawings of
penises. The only thing that seemed worth
documenting was something kind of like an
octopus or a jellyfish, spray painted in black,
its tendrils dragging down through all of the
other tags like mascara being streaked by
tears. I raised my camera to my eye and took
a picture.

Although the door had been chained shut
once, rust had taken care of the need for me
to break an entrance, and the chain hung de-
funct, the door already standing partly open.

The church's windows had been broken out
and boarded up, and there was a hole in the
ceiling that let in cloud-filtered light to catch
what should have been the dust motes that
hung in the air, but the inside of the church
didn't seem dry. It seemed damp and cold,
like the inside of a cave down by the shore.
While the pews were still there, the rest of
the church had been transformed, the walls
hung with all manner of ephemera from the
sea. Shells and dried out starfish and the jaws
of sharks.

The far wall was dark, cast in shadow, and

I raised my camera and popped off the flash. There was a cross, complete with life-size suffering Jesus of the emaciated Catholic variety, that had been broken from its pedestal and leaned against the back wall of the church. There was something wrong with it, though, and I walked closer, raising my camera for another flash.

In place of thorns, Christ now wore a crown of coral on his head, and the body of a giant eel had been wound carefully around his body, secured with the kind of rope that they used to make fishing nets down in the harbor. While the other nautical-themed decorations seemed like they had been out of the sea for a long time, the eel still looked fresh and wet, and smelled like the fish market. I put out my hand, expecting it to suddenly lash and flop at any moment, and when I put my palm against its body it was cold as deep water.

Once I was close enough for my eyes to adjust to the dimness, I could see that there was another bit of graffiti on the wall behind the cross, this one much better than anything that had occupied the door. In it, a dark shape with glowing eyes seemed to be crawling up from somewhere. It was humanoid but

somehow half-formed, soft and overly round-
ed and damp. Stylized fishes swam around its
head, making a halo, or a crown.

I took a bunch of pictures inside the church,
making sure to get plenty of shots of the graffiti and the Jesus wrapped in the eel, wondering as I did if whoever put it there had ever
seen Ken Russell's *Lair of the White Worm*; if
I was looking at some sort of bizarre homage.

Then I just went back outside, got in the
Range Rover, and left. I drove back to the
Cargo Cult, where I had converted a broom
closet into a makeshift darkroom. I developed
the photos there, but I didn't take them to the
sheriff or the paper. What was I going to tell
them? That someone had vandalized the old
church that nobody but punk kids who went
there on dares even cared about anymore?
This didn't have anything to do with the bodies that were washing up. At least, not to the
naked eye.

But I couldn't stop thinking about Blum's
congregation, the way that they had marched
down into the sea with their pockets full of
stones. They were true believers, and I had to
wonder if now they were finally coming back.
Was this Blum's new race of man? Or at least,

the first stage in its evolution?

So I waited for more bodies, more rings of the phone in the middle of the night, though by now I was getting calls from Rudy at the coroner's office more often than the paper, which had decided that my photos were not what they were looking for in this instance and assigned the regular photographer to the job. Still, I went out when I could.

I took to driving up and down the coast road at night, and so I was the first to find the fifth body. Collapsed in an alleyway between the shops that ran along the seawall, not five blocks from the Cargo Cult. It was grown through with coral, and the jellied bodies that filled the caverns of its bones were already starting to decay. "These are the pearls that were his eyes," and all that jazz.

When Sheriff Perkins showed up, he asked me what I was doing out there, and I told him, "Just out for a drive."

It took them six tries before they reached as far as my door. I heard it before I saw it. The wet squeal of damp rubber on glass, a squeegee across your windshield. I was sitting on the couch at the back of the store, not even in my bedroom, and when I looked up, I could see the shape in the doorway. It wasn't like the shape from my dream, not at all, but it *was* familiar. I had seen it painted on the wall of that old church, behind the defaced statue of Christ.

Sort of like a man, but low and oozing. A dark shape that nonetheless glowed. Slime the color of the ocean bed covered it, though within that darkness luminous shadows moved. Its skeleton glowed through, the ribcage, the face, the phalanges of the big, wet hand pressed against the glass. It was as if its bones had been hollowed out, replaced with something bioluminescent from the bottom of the sea. And who knows, perhaps they had?

I stood up from the couch, frozen between stepping forward and running away. There was a back door to the Cargo Cult, an alley and, beyond that, the wooded gulley. But how far would I have to run next time? They had made it farther inland with each excursion, and I didn't think they would be stopping anytime soon.

I don't know now if I really heard the voice, or only imagined it. Dreamed it, standing there in the dark at the back of the store. A wet sound, of course, the squishing of feet in

full galoshes. And yet, there was a familiar-
ity in the voice. It was Rob's voice, it was my
mother's voice, and it said my name from the
other side of the door.

That's what made me walk forward instead
of back, what made me throw the bolt on
the front door and pull it open. And what
collapsed at my feet was nothing more than
a pool of black water and old bones, dead
and dying sea creatures spilling out across
the threadbare carpet in a tidal wave. I stood
there for a long time, waiting to see if something else would come, before I went to the
phone and called the sheriff.

I don't know why it came to the Cargo
Cult. Was it simply because I was close to the
water—I traced a map later, and found that
the video store was smack in the middle of
a beeline course from the beach to the old
church up on the cliff—or was it something
more?

After my nocturnal visitor, I dug through
Rob's piles of old VHS tapes, the ones with
hand-written labels, until I found one that
said "Blum, 73" and below that the words
"New Man." I left it sitting on top of one of
the VCRs while I thought about Rob, about

his ashes spread across the bay. If Blum's congregation had come to the Cargo Cult after
all these years, it had to be for him, not for
me, and he was gone.

The body that came to my door was the
last one that was ever found, though people
continued to report strange things around the
town. Odd noises in the night, pets that went
missing, wet footprints on days when there
had been no rain. Kids in town started claim-
ing that they saw Blum's body hanging from
the bridge, and then even adults were seeing
it, though it was never there whenever they
brought anyone back to look.

The other bodies, the ones that had been
taken to the coroner's office, were dumped
into a pauper's grave in the cemetery out east
of the bay, but they didn't stay there. The
graves were found dug up, the dirt around
them churned into mud, the bodies gone.
Eventually, the sheriff went up to the church
on top of the cliff, on an "unrelated vandal-
ism complaint," and found that it had been
cleaned out. Nothing from the old congregation remained behind, no nautical decorations, no desecrated crucifix. Not even the old
sign out front. A short time later, the church

burned down.

All the while, I stared at that tape sitting on top of the VCR. More than once I went to pick it up, let my fingers rest on it, imagined that it felt cold, like the bottom of the sea. Once I even held it, pushed it against the mouth of the VCR for I don't know how long.

It was something Rob had left behind. Maybe if I put it in, pressed play, it would explain something, or at least let me see him again. But if I watched whatever was on the video, if he had something to do with what was happening, I might judge him, and I had already let him down too completely for that. So, I took it out back, pulled all the tape out, dumped it into a metal garbage can in the alley and set it on fire. My memories of Rob were good; I wanted them to stay that way. I owed him that much, at least.

With the bodies now all gone and the video too, all that was left were my pictures. I sold some of them; not to the *News of the Weird* or anyplace like that, but to a gallery down in Point Reyes, where I haven't ever gone to see them. I can't bear to look at them myself, not anymore. I wonder, in a few dozen years, when the new race of man is ascendant, if I will be seen as a prophet or a traitor to my species. I'm not sure I care too much either way.

No Exit

The landscape of western Kansas lends itself well to conspiracy theories and apocalyptic visions. The plains, vast and windswept, bending imperceptibly to the horizon. The small towns, unmoored from the highway, like ships cast adrift on a fathomless sea of grain, with silos and brick church steeples their only masts.

I saw a lot of it as my parents drove me back and forth after the divorce—my mom moved to Kansas City, my dad to a little town north of Boulder. "The kind of place where you can still get your teeth knocked out by a cowboy, if you put your mind to it," he liked to say. They split custody, so I spent a lot of time in the passenger seat of one car or another, driving those long, blank miles that stretched between the relative civilization of Topeka and Denver.

I spent the school year with my mom, my dad driving into town for the occasional weekend, when we would stay in a hotel and eat ice cream and waffles for just about every meal. During the summer or on holiday breaks, he would pick me up and take me west, stopping at gas stations along the way to buy slushies—"Don't tell your mom," with a conspiratorial wink in my direction—or at the dinosaur museum in Fort Hays. When Mom was driving me back, it was never anything but my forehead pressed against the cool window glass, watching the alternating signs condemning abortion, promising eternal damnation, or advertising sex shops.

When I was a little girl, we had lived in one of those tiny towns that we passed along I-70, with their football fields pressed tight up against the highway. I could remember a house and a yard, a tire swing hanging from the branches of a tree, the golden sunlight and skin-flaying wind that came with life out in the western plains. I could remember my older sister Danielle, only barely. She was a blur of brown hair and freckles, as tall as my mom, with a barking laugh that seemed to echo.

I was six years old when she died, and my parents divorced within seven months. Years later, I would look up the divorce rates for couples who have lost a child and find that it was much lower than I had been led to believe by counselors and self-help books. Only about sixteen percent, and most of them said that there were problems in the marriage long before the child died. Were there problems in my parents' marriage? I never asked and they never told me.

Of course, Danielle didn't just die, either. That would have been one thing. This was something much worse.

***

While snake handlers and the like tend to stay down in Oklahoma and farther south, western Kansas has been home to more than its fair share of fire-and-brimstone revivals, to preachers spewing admonitions about the end of days, not to mention less prosaic cults. The people who planned the bombings of abortion clinics in Wichita in 1993 got their start here, and so did Edward Murray and his "dynamo-electric messiah," and the Increase

Brothers, who claimed that the Garden of Eden had, in fact, been located just a few miles outside of the little town of Lebanon, Kansas.

And, of course, most infamously, Damien Hesher and the Spiritus Aetum Sperarum, which Hesher claimed translated to the Breath of the Spheres, though that's probably a little loose. The Spiritus would have been a nothing cult, a footnote in the history of the region's odd beliefs, had it not been for one afternoon in 1987, when Hesher and a bunch of his cronies kidnapped a bus full of seven high school kids and their coach as it was on its way back from a debate championship in Manhattan, Kansas. One of those kids was Danielle.

Hesher and his followers forced her and the others into a beat-up RV, leaving the bus driver where he sat on the shoulder of I-70, with the added gift of a sucking chest wound from a double-barrel shotgun. Then they drove to a little rest stop west of Topeka, situated on a limestone outcropping where I-70 split, its top crowned with spidery scrub trees.

That rest stop was where my sister died, and we drove past it every time my parents ferried me back and forth from Kansas City to Colorado. By that time, though, the turn-off leading to it had been stoppered with blue wooden sawhorses and concrete blocks that had previously been highway dividers; the brown sign that once said "Rest Stop" plastered over with other official signage, white with black letters spelling out two simple words: NO EXIT.

***

Maybe it would have been enough if Hesher and his followers had just killed the handful of kids they took from that bus. Certainly, it would have made the national news, maybe even gotten a few books written about it. But it probably wouldn't have closed down the rest stop forever. It took something special for that.

The kids weren't just killed. They were torn apart. Limbs and guts and heads and whatever else strewn all over the place, like something from a Halloween haunted house. They say that the blood soaked into the parking area and wouldn't ever come clean.

At least one of the kids threw themselves

from the limestone cliff and smashed on the rocks below rather than face whatever reckoning was taking place at that rest stop. The coach managed to crawl some twenty yards from the parked RV where the slaughter began, albeit leaving parts of his legs behind as he did.

The crime scene photos were all dark and blurry. They reminded me of photos of bigfoot or cattle mutilations; nothing in them identifiable except by its vague shape. The RV parked in the lot of the rest stop, and on its door, painted in what looked like blood, an image of a circle being pierced by a line from above.

Not all the bodies were ever even accounted for, and there was a period of time when the police entertained the idea that some of the kids had managed to escape, that they might just show up, bloodstained and in shock, standing by the side of the highway. A time when Danielle was simply "missing" instead of "presumed dead."

It's impossible not to wonder how the story would have gone differently if Hesher and his crew had survived to stand trial, but when authorities arrived they found Hesher and all of his followers dead inside the RV, symbols carved into their skin, their throats cut.

"Murder/suicide" was the official conclusion, though I found a coroner's report that had been excised from the public record—performed, according to the official account, by a junior medical examiner who had been too shaken by the grisly scene to render an accurate verdict—that said Hesher and his people had died sometime *before* most of the other victims.

Even leaving that report aside, it was difficult to square up the crime scene with the murders themselves. Though obvious acts of cannibalism had been performed on the victims, no human remains were found in the digestive tracts of either Hesher or his followers. For a while, the authorities sought other accomplices who had fled the scene rather than participate in the cult's mass suicide, eventually chalking the partially-devoured state of the bodies up to the depredations of scavengers.

My parents never talked about what happened; not with reporters, and not with me. If they ever talked about it between themselves—as I know they must have—I never overheard it. I would wonder later if they were trying to protect me by never speaking of it. The Satanic Panic was still going strong when the murders were committed, and there was a media frenzy surrounding the slaughter for months, with local and national news stations trotting out stories of animal sacrifices, kidnappings that predated the murders, and, of course, other, more salacious stuff. A few years later, *Unsolved Mysteries* even ran a segment and called my parents, who refused to comment or appear on the show.

Being in the crosshairs of that kind of hyperbolic attention would be hard enough on grieving parents, let alone a confused kid. Maybe by the time public interest in the murders faded, my parents had decided that it was easier to ignore what had happened than it was to face it, leaving me alone to take the opposite route.

The proximity of the murders were what kept me at KU when I went to college, even though my dad could have gotten me reduced tuition at CU Boulder, where he was teaching by then. From KU, I could go around to those local stations that were still extant and go through their archives for any old footage about the murders. I probably read every newspaper article ever printed on the subject; police reports, autopsies, anything that I could get my hands on.

When my parents divorced, my mom switched my name and hers back to her maiden name, and though she changed hers again when she married a man named Dale years later, I kept the old one, so there was nothing left to tie me to Danielle in most peoples' eyes. I could check out books about the murders from the library, request newspaper stories on microfiche, ask around at news stations, and nobody would think I was anything but a morbid kid with a curiosity about a grisly local crime that had taken on the proportions of urban myth.

Most of the time, anyone who reported on the killings was content to conjecture wildly about Hesher's motives and the beliefs and practices of the Spiritus Aetum Sperarum. Hardly anyone bothered to read the admittedly nigh-unreadable book that Hesher had written and self-published, under the unhelpful title *Wizard's Ashes*.

The book cover was simple, dominated by a drawing of a red circle being pierced by a line from above, done in a style like calligraphy. That was on the original edition. After the murders, it was picked back up by a small press called Hex Books and reissued under a new title—*The Breath of the Spheres: Secrets of the Spiritus Aetum Sperarum*—which attempted to market it as a "true" book of dark spirituality, in order to cash in on the notoriety generated by Hesher's crimes. That book's cover featured a blurry and distorted photo of Hesher himself, as he had been found by police when they raided the RV: A cow skull on his head that had been denuded of its horns and carved out inside so that it covered his face like a mask.

That was the version I read, complete with typographical errors and pages that didn't always line up correctly with the margins. It contained a brief, and completely fictitious, biographical sketch of Damien Hesher in the "About the Author" portion at the back of the book. In reality, Damien Hesher had been born in Topeka, and had lived his entire life in Kansas. Starting out as Jeremy Miller, he had legally changed his name when he turned twenty-one, the same time he started the Spiritus Aetum Sperarum. All that I learned from other sources. From his book, I learned that the place where my sister was murdered hadn't been chosen randomly.

While Hesher's book didn't lay out the specifics of the killing spree, it was full of distressing hints. Hesher was clearly obsessed with the rest stop, which he referred to in the book not only by number but by latitude and longitude. He called it a "thin place," and said that it was somewhere that "communion" was possible, if the proper sacrifice was on hand.

According to Hesher, it wasn't the first time that blood had been spilled on that very ground. In the book he told a story about a family called the Millers—no accident, perhaps, that they shared his own born surname—who had diverged from the Oregon trail and found themselves on that same limestone outcropping where the rest stop would eventually be built.

By Hesher's account, their wagon wheel broke on that spot and they didn't have another one to replace it. What led them from that predicament to what came next is unclear, but he wrote that they took the broken wheel and laid it on the ground, and from there they drew lines, extending the spokes of the wheel outward and outward, decorating them with orbs, sometimes drawn in the dirt, sometimes represented by the smoothest rocks they could find in the surrounding cliffs and gullies. Then, they sat down among the lines and spheres, and they ate themselves. Not the desperate, no-other-choice cannibalism of the Donner party. Intentional, premeditated anthropophagy.

The *why* of it was tougher to pin down than the what. Hesher's writing was rambling, inconsistent, littered with typos and odd grammatical choices, the voice constantly changing, as though the book had been written by diverse hands. What was clear was that Hesher believed that the earth was filled with what he sometimes called "abysses" and other times "spheres."

"Not hollow," he wrote, "as an egg might be hollow, but carved out, digged full of holes, as a cork, or a nest." There was no heaven or hell, according to Hesher. No higher power, and no lower one, but in these holes there were *entities* who could do things, and sometimes they would whisper to those of us who lived above, as they had to the Millers, as they did to him.

These were what he was planning to "commune" with when he killed my sister and her classmates. "Eternity is a cruel thing," he wrote, "but long lastingness is within our grasp, if we are willing to sacrifice much. Being a man is a thing that we can easily cast off, if we are willing to reach past our own bodies to what lies beneath.

"What scuttles in the shadows when the light of the sun is turned off? Why would we dream that we have seen but the tip of its great limb? It is in the shadow of the world, and it is in the shadow of our hearts. If we open ourselves up to the breath of the abyss, we will hear it whisper our name."

***

Given my preoccupation with the circumstances of Danielle's death, I don't know why it took me so long to go to the crime scene. By the time I did I had graduated from college, taking a job as a file clerk at a Kansas City law firm, pushing wheeled carts down long aisles in the dim basement of a tall building. My dad had been in and out of the hospital with colon cancer, and I had driven my old Passat out to Boulder easily more than a dozen times to visit him, passing by the rest stop and the NO EXIT sign each time I did.

I think maybe I put off visiting it because I knew that there wouldn't be anything left after that. Danielle was gone, Hesher and his people were in the ground. I had read everything I could find, watched everything there was to watch. My parents never spoke about it, and I never got up the nerve to ask. The rest stop would be the last place I could go to feel closer to Danielle, to make her something more than a fading memory.

"Legend tripping" is what they call it, I guess, and I could tell before I saw much else that I wasn't the first to make the journey. I moved the blue painted sawhorses but parked my Passat next to the chunks of concrete, hiking the rest of the way up to the top of the limestone hill, topped with a line of scrub trees that circled it like a crown.

From the highway, the restroom building and the rotted remains of the picnic shelters didn't look much different from their brethren at other, less-neglected stops. Up close, though, I could see that they had been visited by graffiti in all its varied forms, from pentagrams and inverted crosses to swastikas, declarations of love, and crude drawings of male and female genitalia.

Some aspiring graffiti artist had even done their homework. A red circle pierced by a line was spray-painted onto the sidewalk directly in front of the restrooms, in the spot where you would stand to look at the map behind the plexiglass, if such a map were still present, instead of an empty box with webs in the corners and the dried-up bodies of dead spiders collecting at the bottom.

In the light of the setting sun, I could see stains on the overgrown parking lot, though whether they were made by oil or blood it was impossible to tell. Some of the picnic shelters were missing their roofs, others their picnic tables. All of them had suffered more from the years of neglect than the restrooms had, the wood splintering and breaking apart while the tan brick of the restroom building simply faded.

The door marked "WOMEN" was oddly difficult to open—like there was something behind it, holding it shut, but not anything substantial. Shining my flashlight into the dark on the other side, I saw why.

The restroom had probably never been very tidy or welcoming. It was the same as the ones in every other rest stop I had ever visited: concrete floors, windows set high in the walls to let in what little light could force its way past the dust-coated plexiglass, a trio of metal stalls and boxy troughs for sinks. I knew such rest stop bathrooms well from my many pilgrimages along I-70, and was familiar with them as homes for dead leaves, dead bugs, cobwebs, and dust. But this one was positively *festooned* with spider webs.

It was as if the decorator for an old Gothic horror film had gone to town but had never been told to stop. The webs filled the room with such proliferation as to make no sense. No insect could ever penetrate them deeply enough for any but the ones nearest the door to catch any prey, and yet they filled every space, the strands sometimes the monofilament thickness that I was used to in spider's webs, other times reaching a ropy girth that called to mind alien slime or the webs of mutant spiders from the movies.

These were what had made forcing the door open feel like fighting my way past marshmallow fluff, and as I flashed my light across the sticky strands, I thought I saw something writhing in their depths. Something much too big to be an insect, and too malformed to be human. It let out a mewling sound, and I stumbled back, the door swinging shut behind me.

Or had I gone through a door, after all? The light on the other side seemed changed in some subtle way, the setting sun painting the sky with the radiation glow of a post-apocalyptic future. That wasn't all that had changed, either. There was an RV in the parking lot that hadn't been there before. One that looked all too familiar, down to the circle being pierced by the line daubed onto the door in something too dark to be paint.

All around me, it seemed that the trees were moving closer whenever I wasn't looking. I imagined them turning upside-down, their branches becoming spidery legs on which they crept nearer, only to plant themselves again, head down in the dirt, whenever my eyes swept across them. For all that I told myself it was a panic response, a trick of the mind, there was no denying that when I looked again what had been thirty paces from the picnic shelters became twenty, twenty became ten.

With the trees closing in, I don't know why I thought the RV was a safer place to be, but I found myself standing in front of its door nevertheless.

On the other side I could hear sounds. Voices whispering, and something else. The sound of a dozen blades sawing flesh. The door had a handle, the kind that turns downward, a line piercing a circle into the earth, and I turned it and the door opened outward, and from inside came the reptile house smell of pennies and fresh soil.

Inside was Damien Hesher. On his head he wore that same cow skull, its teeth and horns missing, transforming it into something else, the helmet of a cyclops, the head of an insect. On his hands he wore claws made from the bones of small animals; the same claws he had used, according to the coroner's report, to tear out his own throat, though I saw now that those claws were unstained by blood.

His neck was still a bloody, ragged wound, though something now moved inside it, working open and closed. "Eternity is a cruel thing," are the only words he said to me, the sounds coming not from where his mouth should have been, but from the ragged hole in his neck. Then *they* came for him.

The floor of the RV opened like a series of trap doors held tight by webbing, the seams invisible until triggered. Black limbs rose up from the floor, scuttling bodies like the ones I had imagined attached to the spidery trees. They embraced Damien Hesher, taking him back with them to wherever it was he now resided.

The hand that he reached out toward me was not threatening but supplicating. Beneath those claws of bone, the pad of his hand was pink and soft. I felt sorry for him, this man who had thought he could peer into a dark well and not be frightened by what he saw. I stumbled back, as more of the dark shapes came surging up from the glowing trap doors, and felt a hand fall on my shoulder.

She stood behind me, still as tall as my mom. She wore the same jeans and hoodie that she had worn when she disappeared, but the hand that touched me wasn't anything I recognized, and in the dark shadows of that hood her eyes seemed to glitter, and a seam split her face, running up her neck, up her chin. Her smile was the same, though, and she said my name as my arms went around her and I pressed my face into her shoulder, realizing only as I did so that I had gotten to be just as tall as her, over the years.

When I could no longer feel her arms around me, I opened my eyes, and found myself standing in the parking lot of the rest stop, my shoes on the asphalt. The RV was gone. The sun had set completely, and the night sky was filled with stars, the stunted trees having retreated to their usual distance, though I had the feeling it was only a temporary armistice, not a permanent peace.

When I got back to my Passat and sat down in the driver's seat, I felt something crinkle in my back pocket. Pulling it out, I found a faded polaroid of me and Danielle. I was sitting in front of her on the brass bed I had when I was little, and she was braiding my hair and smiling, her face suddenly clarified in the blur of my memory.

Looking up, I thought I saw her watching me from the tree line, those black eyes sparkling, but when I shut off the dome light there was nothing there. Just the fading hint of a door closing in the rocky cliffside, maybe, nothing more.

LEANDRA'S STORY

When they dug up the makeshift grave and found him gone, there were titters of nervous laughter from the crowd. Because maybe this was supposed to be the trick, right? And it was, it was, but still, Leandra knew that something was wrong, even before they pried open the lid and found the casket empty, as it should have been, but the back panel still hanging open into darkness, in a way that he never would have left it.

Ice water was already coursing through her veins before she saw that gaping doorway into the earth, but that was the moment when her heart dropped, when all the air in her lungs just disappeared, replaced by an aching vacuum that left her gasping.

Even then, she kept half-expecting him to come popping out from behind some tombstone, to appear on the roof of a nearby crypt shouting "Surprise!" Waiting for it as the moment stretched, dragged, became moments, plural, then hours, then days. As the nervous laughter of the crowd turned to anger, to distress. As the onlookers thinned, replaced with the strobing red-and-blue lights of emergency vehicles.

Godfrey did his best to placate them, to keep them away from her, shifting almost mechanically into the role that he had always played. As the sun sank, she felt someone drape a heavy blanket across her shoulders and realized that she hadn't moved from the spot where she had been standing when they opened the casket. She was rooted there, like a beetle pinned to a board by a giant needle.

They went down into the hole, of course. Godfrey and the police and that kid Scott had just hired back in the summer, Robert pronounced "Row-bear." The tunnel was still there, the one that they had dug days before, leading from the makeshift grave to a nearby crypt with a secret panel that would allow Scott to make his triumphant reappearance, take his bows, accept the applause of the gathered crowd. But now another tunnel

joined with it, one that Godfrey assured her
had not been there when they dug their own
escape route.

"It seemed older," he said, the implied rest
of the sentence hanging unspoken in the air:
than it could have been.

The second tunnel extended only a short
distance before stopping. Not in more graveyard earth but in ancient masonry, the foundation of a crypt sunk deep into the soil. Not
something that anyone, even a magician,
could have erected on short notice.

Leandra wanted to go with them down into
the dark, but she couldn't. She just stood in
that one spot, allowing Godfrey to speak for
her when he could, answering questions with
only a nod or a shake of her head, when she
heard them at all.

It wasn't until she had been loaded into the
hearse that they drove out to the graveyard
as part of the show, the one where they kept
the trick coffin; until she had been deposited
back at the house, Godfrey standing in the
porch light and asking her over and over if
she was sure she was okay, could he come in,
fix her anything, bring her anything; until she
had collapsed on the couch and realized that

the scratchy EMT blanket was still draped over her shoulders that she finally felt the pain flooding into her legs from standing in one place for so very long.

Maybe she slept some that night, in that spot on the couch, or maybe she just lay there in the ever-encroaching dark, eyes open, pupils wide to catch the little flickers of light, until the sun rose through the big windows.

Godfrey was on her porch again that morning; the ring of the doorbell, the chimes that Scott had picked out when the house was built, and Godfrey's dark, bald head seen through the glass at the side of the door. He asked her how she had slept, was there anything he could do. He asked her about coffee—for her, not for him—and she shook her head, the blanket still draped over her like a mantle. He told her that the police were going back to search again that day, but the way he said it, she could hear in his voice that he hoped she would stay at home. "Will you go for me?" she asked, knowing that it was what he wanted to hear.

When he left, she went back to the couch and sat until the pain in her throat and tongue sent her stumbling to the kitchen. Her mouth tasted like she had been eating cigarette butts all night, though she hadn't smoked a cigarette in three years. Scott had asked her to stop, so she had stopped.

She got a glass from the cabinet and filled it from the refrigerator, her hand shaking so that she sloshed water into the drip tray and the slate-tiled floor. She drank the whole glass in one long gulp, her throat working as she swallowed, and the cold water hit her stomach like oil and she thought that she might be sick in the kitchen sink.

For a while she just stood there, glass on the counter, hands on either side of the sink, shoulder blades spiked up like the wings of an angel about to unfurl. Her dark hair was coming loose from the bun she wore it in when Scott was performing, strands clouding the edges of her vision as she held her head over the sink. Her knees wobbled as she hung there, feeling sick, feeling a bottomless emptiness in the caverns of her belly that rejected the cold water. Rejected anything but their own concavity, their ache.

After a long time, she spat into the sink, then turned on the tap and watched it swirl her spit down the drain, then splashed cold water on her face.

Somewhere between the kitchen and the master bathroom she lost the EMT blanket. Later, she would find it in a pile near the top of the stairs. She brushed her teeth and stood under the near-boiling water that poured out of the shower head. Felt it cooking her shoulders and the tops of her breasts red. When she had toweled off she pulled on a robe, as though she was going to go back downstairs, do something that might have helped, instead of lying on top of the covers and staring up at the white ceiling, waiting for the dark to come again.

When three days had passed and Scott had not reappeared—stepping out of the second-story closet or coming nonchalantly up the basement stairs whistling that tune—Leandra went back out to the graveyard. She called a car, rather than calling Godfrey, and had the driver wait in it while she got out.

Yellow police tape fluttered in a chilly breeze under overcast skies, but no cruisers were there and any crowd had long since dispersed. The grave had been filled back in, the dirt mounded up on top, light and reddish, but the prop gravestone was still there: HERE LIES SCOTT CANDISH, PATIENTLY AWAITING RESURRECTION.

She ducked under the police tape and let her hand rest on the headstone. It wasn't really granite or marble; a light facsimile, like the kind they used in movies, it felt a bit like heavy foam under her fingers. From there, with measured steps, keeping her eyes on the grass just in front of her feet, she walked the path that the tunnel would have taken. First the one that they had dug, hardly a tunnel at all, just big enough for Scott to wiggle through. Three paces back from the grave, nine over to the door of the crypt.

The crypt itself was real enough. Scott had paid the family a few thousand to let him cut a secret panel, use their great-grandfather's resting place as part of his gimmick. Inside had been a change of clothes, an identical suit to the one that Scott had been wearing when he was laid into the coffin, but not stained with dirt from his crawl through the dark.

Standing on the stone step, she put her hand against the metal door of the crypt. The police had already been inside, with Godfrey. They had collected Scott's clothes, which were right where he had left them. The secret door hadn't been used, that's what Godfrey said, and Leandra trusted him. She didn't need to push through the crypt door to see for herself. Besides, if Scott was going to disappear, he had too much experience with magic to do it in the very place where his audience would be looking.

Leandra turned around and walked back to the point where Godfrey said the other tunnel had intersected theirs. It was bigger, he said, almost large enough for him to stand up straight, and he had never been a short man. It extended only a short distance before dead-ending at the wall of the other crypt.

She followed the path of the tunnel to the wall, then followed the wall around to its front, which faced away from the scene of the disastrous trick. This could have been an escape route, had Scott been able to get through the underground wall, which Godfrey assured her was impossible. But then, when he was first starting out, wasn't Scott's tagline SCOTT CANDISH MAKES THE IMPOSSIBLE POSSIBLE?

This crypt was even older than the other, the name above the door eaten away by lichens and by time. She tried it, but the verdigris-green metal was padlocked shut. Was there an answering sound on the other side? A scratching? If so, she wasn't yet crazy enough to break into a strange crypt on the off chance that she *wasn't* hearing things. Instead, she walked back to the car, drove back to the house in the hills.

The police came a few times over the next few days. Two officers, in uniforms. Not even detectives, not plainclothes. A woman named Paula—wide-faced, her hair held back in a ponytail—and a younger man, black with a heavy brow. He talked less than she did, said his name was Oscar.

Leandra had never met anyone named Oscar, and told him so. "My mom loved Sesame Street," he said, without any hint of a smile to show whether he was joking or not.

They took up space in her living room—Paula up and pacing, Oscar sitting on the corner of the off-white couch, up near the edge. She offered them coffee, which Oscar accepted. They asked her questions; about her relationship with Scott, about the mechanics of the trick.

"You should ask Godfrey," she told them in response to the latter. Godfrey and Scott had always worked the tricks together. Since before she met him, before Scott was famous, a household name, or as close as magicians ever got these days. Back when it was just the two of them doing lame tricks at high school talent shows. She had seen the pictures. She figured the police had, too.

"Can you think of any reason why your husband might have left?" Paula asked, pacing. Oscar sat on the couch, sipping his coffee—two sugars, actual cubes fished out of a bowl on the kitchen table, which Leandra had stirred in, clinking the spoon against the ceramic cup.

"Had you two been fighting?" Oscar clarified. "We hate to ask, but…"

"Was there anyone else in his life?" Paula asked, when Oscar let the rest of his sentence just fade in the air, like vanishing contrails in the Nevada sky.

It wasn't as if Scott had been lacking in opportunities to stray. Magicians weren't exactly rock stars in this day and age, but they did live and work in Las Vegas, after all. But how to tell these police officers in their bulky

uniforms about what Scott was like? How
fragile he was? How troubled by bad dreams?
How long it had taken him to let her sleep
beside him, even months after the first time
they made love? How lucky she had felt that
night, when he curled against her in his sleep?
How he still sometimes recoiled at even a
gentle touch?

Sitting there, in her own living room, trying to imagine explaining that to people who
only knew Scott from his stage presence, if
they knew him at all, made her angry, and she
actually welcomed that stirring of heat in her
breast, the first thing besides a hollow ache
that she had felt in days.

Leandra hadn't been Scott's first box jump-
er, and she wasn't his last, but she was the
only one to become his business manager,
and then his wife. While he and Godfrey
had been friends since high school, Leandra
liked to think that she knew Scott better than
anyone else, that she would have known if he
was unhappy with her, with his life. But she
couldn't deny that if he wanted to disappear,
well, he *was* a magician, after all. It was one
thing he certainly knew how to do.

It wasn't as if she hadn't entertained the

same thoughts that the police were now pushing around in their minds. Staring out the big windows at the low, distant skyline or the manufactured landscape painstakingly sculpted out of the Nevada desert, she had tried to picture him in some anonymous hotel room, rolling around in the blankets with some new young girl, or in some nameless bar in Cancun with dark sunglasses and a suitcase full of cash.

She had even tried to imagine him cold and dead, lying waxy on the slab in a morgue someplace where nobody recognized his face from posters or TV specials, where nobody knew his name. None of these scenarios provided her with any comfort, but she tortured herself with them all the same.

She knew how all of this looked to the police: Magician disappears in the midst of ridiculous stunt, leaves wife holding the bag. They thought that he was another flighty celebrity caught, perhaps, in some midlife crisis or, at worst, some kind of financial trouble. Maybe he liked to gamble, was into drugs or prostitutes. Maybe he got in deep with the wrong people.

"We'll do everything we can," one of the

officers said as they left, Leandra standing in the doorway until they had climbed back into their cruiser, but she knew that they had already stopped looking.

When Scott had been gone for a month, they had a funeral. An empty black coffin with gold trim was lowered down into the dirt and she stood apart from the crowd, under the shade of a black umbrella, though there wasn't a cloud in the sky. Her hair was up in a bun, the way she wore it when Scott was working, and she had on a coat and dark glasses. She noticed photographers snapping her picture but ignored them, wondering how bored people would have to be to pick up some tabloid rag because it had her grieving picture on the front.

The stone was a faintly rose-colored marble—Godfrey had picked it out, ultimately. When she had tried she'd found herself sobbing and saying, "Why don't we just use the stupid foam one from the trick?"

It said Scott Candish and his birth date and then a dash and a blank space. Below that was "Husband & Magician," and Leandra said a mental thank-you to Godfrey that the one came before the other, though she also thought that, probably, that was backwards. Next to his name, there was a space for hers. She couldn't decide if that was sweet or morbid. Maybe both.

After the eulogy, and the coffin was lowered down into the ground, people came in a seemingly unending line to pay their respects. They dropped flowers, touched the gravestone. They had tears in their eyes, leaving crystalline trails down their cheeks, but Leandra didn't recognize most of them. This was the irony of celebrity, even a petty celebrity like the one Scott had enjoyed. You touched so deeply the lives of people whose faces you never saw.

Could any of them have imagined him, starting awake in the night, his frame dewy with sweat, his eyes dark holes in a mask? Could they have reconciled his voice, which reverberated with such authority from the stage, with the one who begged her not to leave him alone in the dark. "Don't let them touch me," he pleaded, his voice was that of a child, not a man.

That night, Leandra had a bad dream of her own. It began at the graveyard, just as it had been that day, but she was alone, rather than surrounded by fans and photographers. The graveyard didn't look quite the same, either. It was the graveyard from the trick, though the headstone was the rose-colored marble. Gravediggers were filling the grave in with shovels, even though she knew that in real life they used a backhoe, and she stood there, wincing as each shovelful hit the black casket.

Then she was seeing inside the casket. It was like the graveyard was a model, and the side had been cut away. She could see the dirt, see the white lining of the coffin. A door was opening in the back of the coffin. Pink light poured through, like the vacancy sign at a roadside motel. The door was small, but Scott was coming through it nonetheless, his arms and legs in the suit that he had disappeared in, bunching up through the opening, like a crushed bug.

He was inside now, settling himself as if for sleep, crossing his arms over his chest, closing his eyes. She could still hear the sound of the dirt falling on the roof, but now her point-of-view was trapped inside the coffin with Scott. She wanted to yell at him, to pound her fists against him, to bang on the coffin lid and demand that the gravediggers stop, stop, stop what they were doing because he was still alive, but she was powerless, voiceless, incorporeal.

The pink glow faded and she opened her eyes. For a moment she could still hear the shovelfuls of dirt falling, and then she realized that it was rain pelting the roof of their house in the hills.

By then, she had already resumed control over the business. Making phone calls, signing checks, cancelling engagements, paying bills. Everyone was patient and understanding at first, but both were beginning to fray by the time a month had gone by. Tickets had to be refunded. Venues were upset. Godfrey tried to screen the most taxing duties, but she was the one who had power of attorney, so often her signature was the one that was required.

After the nightmare, she sat on the side of the bed—the side that Scott had always slept on now cold from his absence—and held the receiver of the phone in her hand until it began to beep insistently at her. She was thinking about calling Godfrey, having him disinter the empty coffin so that she could open it and see for herself that Scott hadn't somehow magically appeared inside.

"Magically," how he had hated that word, when applied to what he did. "This isn't even illusion," he would say, knocking on some hollow box or other gizmo designed for his latest trick. "Not prestidigitation. I'm more like an athlete than a conjurer. I dress it up in mummery and quasi-religious awe because I'm expected to, but what I'm doing, *all* I'm doing, is a fancy bit of sleight of hand—sometimes sleight of whole body. But it's no more magical than a gymnast doing an impressive handstand. I can't do what they're doing, but that doesn't make it magic. It just means they've practiced."

It wasn't a way to be down on himself—though certainly he had those, too. It was simply that he believed that the word magic should be reserved for something more. "I want to believe that there's something magic out there, don't you?" he asked her, on the night they first made love. "My grandfather sure believed it. That there was more to the world than these four corners. I guess that's the appeal of faith."

She had told him about her Nana, who had

candles of the saints, hung chicken feet up in her kitchen, talked about the loa, about root work and other things. Scott had a huge library of occult books, and she had read enough of them to know that her Nana was practicing some kind of pidgin of different beliefs, but that hadn't made it any less real to her.

"Did *you* believe it?" he asked her, and she said that she didn't really know.

"I knew that she did," Leandra said. "It was real for her, and that was enough for me. Does that make any sense?"

"Yeah," Scott said, and stared up at the ceiling the way he did sometimes, when he was remembering, "it does."

When he had been gone for six weeks, she got into the silver Lexus and drove the seven hours up I-15 to the little unincorporated town in the hills north of Ogden where Scott had grown up. Her phone buzzed in the cup holder as she was passing Salt Lake City, and she knew that it was Godfrey, but she ignored it.

There wasn't any kind of sign at the city limits, BIRTHPLACE OF SCOTT CANDISH or anything like that. Scott hadn't ever really talked about it much, and they had been back only once during the years that they were married, even though he still owned the property. They flew in to Salt Lake City to attend his father's funeral, and afterward Scott had driven her up into the hills, still dressed in his charcoal-gray funeral suit, and taken her to see the little boxy house where he had grown up.

The town itself was called Galilee and amounted to little more than a cluster of houses, shops, and a fire station in a sheet metal building, all relying on their relative proximity to Ogden to remain viable. From some parts of town, you could see the Pineview Reservoir, but not from Scott's old house. Compared to their current home in Vegas, the place was a shoebox, though when she was younger, Leandra had lived in apartments that were much smaller.

When Scott brought her to the house after his father's funeral, it had already been closed up for years. Scott and his parents had moved to Salt Lake City when Scott was in fifth grade, and had lived there until first his mother and then his father passed away. The house in Galilee had sat empty and, when Scott walked her through it, the rooms had mostly been vacant, those few bits of furniture that remained draped in old bedsheets.

"Stuff that belonged to my grandpa," Scott had said, as they walked through the ghostly rooms. "It wouldn't fit in our place in Salt Lake."

She had never asked him why he didn't sell the house. Not then, and not in the years during which she managed most of his finances. Each person who orbited Scott had a role in his life; he was that kind of person. Hers wasn't to ask him why he did the things he did, why he was the man he was. Hers was to smooth down his hair, to kiss him on the forehead.

For as long as she had known him, Scott had suffered from terrible nightmares, but they grew worse in the weeks and months following his father's death. "He's wearing the suit that we buried him in," he told her once, sitting up in bed in the wash of cold light from the desert moon outside. "That's how I know it's him. He's standing at the foot of my bed. Not this one, the one I slept in when I was a kid, before we moved to Salt Lake. He's too short, though. He barely sticks up above the footboard."

She had tried to hold him, but he flicked her hands away, just short of striking at her, the way he did when he couldn't stand to be touched. "I know it's him because of the suit, but his face isn't right. It isn't his face at all. It's like a spider, or a frog."

"But spiders and frogs don't look anything alike," she attempted to object.

"I know that," he said. "Just let me tell it."

That had always been her role. To let him tell it. Their story had always really been *his* story, and that had been enough for her. More than enough, in fact. It had taken the pressure off. She didn't have to be the sun, because she could be his moon. Because, when you got right down to it, she didn't think there really *was* much to her story, and she didn't care much for what was there.

Scott was the star, the genius, and she was happy to be there to support him, to wait in the wings after the show, to stand in the shadow of his brilliance.

Without that shadow, though, she wasn't sure what to do with herself anymore.

***

The little town of Galilee looked much as she remembered it from her one previous trip—cold and somehow abandoned up here in the bowl of the hills. There were maybe fewer open storefronts than there had been last time, and those that remained seemed to have become somewhat more colorful as practical shops were slowly subsumed by boutiques run by people who didn't need to earn a regular living.

"Snow used to close the roads sometimes, in the winter," Scott had told her, the last time they were here. "Then we were stuck and we had to eat whatever we could get from the local grocer, and they had to sell whatever they had, because trucks couldn't get through. We ate a lot of Vienna sausages and Spam those days. My mom used to fry it in the skillet, and sometimes I still crave it."

She drove by the grocer's—that's all the sign said, G-R-O-C-E-R-S in separate block letters, but Scott always called it Darnell's—and the handful of cars in the parking lot. Turned at one of the few corners in town, and drove to where the old house still sat.

The yard was mowed—their accountant sent a check to a local man twice a year to keep it that way—and the house had that for-lorn look about it that comes when a place is still in fine enough repair, but you can never-theless tell that it is abandoned.

The walls had been painted within the last few years, by the same man who mowed the lawn, but the paint color chosen had an odd-ly fungal pallor that made the house look pale and wan. Sickly. Sitting in the driveway, there was nothing to indicate that the house was anything out of the ordinary. Except for the fact that the lot on which it sat was slightly larger than the others on this block, there was no way to distinguish it from the other houses around it. Nothing about it to suggest that it was the childhood home of someone famous—of someone she loved. Nothing to set it apart at all, except for the shed.

A low, chain link fence encircled the back yard and, with it, the shed. It had been made of wood once, and she guessed it still was un-derneath, but Scott's father had encased it in a shell of corrugated metal after Scott's grand-father died. It sat at the end of the drive, and would have looked like a garage had it boasted more than a single, regular-sized metal door, held shut with a padlock that was still shiny silver, suggesting either that Scott had been here more recently than she realized, or that the man who mowed the lawns had also been tasked at some point with changing the locks.

In front of the shed, in the middle of the yard, were two square wooden posts, each about a foot high. They had been cut off with a chainsaw long enough ago that they now looked uniformly weathered, as though they had been driven into the lawn there just as odd decorations. There was nothing left except their unusual placement next to each other to indicate that they had ever been a sign, advertising for the Church of Inner Light.

His grandfather's church wasn't something that Scott had talked about often. "I don't really even remember it," he said to her when she asked. "He had closed it down by the time I was born, was already just an irascible old man who walked around with a cane and said weird things. There weren't many old men in town who *didn't* say weird things, you know?"

When Scott's father put up the sheet metal shell, he also put up the padlock, and he forbade Scott from going inside, telling him that the place was full of deadly brown recluse spiders, whose bite could cause your skin to rot, like leprosy. It wasn't until years later that Scott would learn that that recluses didn't generally live that far north, and that the far more likely culprits were decidedly less deadly hobo spiders.

Not that the change in genus made Scott any more likely to enter the shed. By the time he was old enough to be curious and dexterous enough to find a way past the padlock, his father had already successfully transmitted his own severe arachnophobia to his son.

She remembered when they first moved in together, her finding a spider skittering along the edge of the sink. She had tried to capture it with a cup and a sheet of paper, but before she could get back with the paper it was crushed beneath Scott's glass. "I'm sorry," he said. "I know it's cruel. I just... I can't stand the idea of them in the house."

She told him it was okay, scooped the smooshed body with its curled-up legs onto the sheet of paper, and went to dump it down the sink. "Not there," Scott said. "Please. Throw it outside. If it goes down the drain, then I'll imagine its black little legs crawling back up."

So she threw it out the back door, where *she* imagined thousands of tiny red ants coming to rend it apart and carry it down into their own dens beneath the earth, retribution for all the insects the spider had consumed over the years. Nature red in tooth and claw, all that jazz.

In the console of the car was a ring of keys that she had taken from Scott's desk drawer. On it were the keys to this place, the front and back doors of the house and the padlock on the door of the shed.

When it had been in operation, the Church of Inner Light had seated the handful of parishioners who came from Ogden and points beyond to hear Tobias Candish's sermons about the Hollow Earth. That's what the church was, at least to hear Scott tell it. Not some odd Evangelical Christian sect, not even spiritualists, but some kind of weird nonsense about golden cities under the ground, where people lived alongside dinosaurs in a land of eternal light.

She had seen the gravestone in Salt Lake City, where Scott's grandfather had been buried. What had it said? "And I will go down the steps that have been cut for me from the stone of the Earth, and there I will find the place that has been prepared for me."

Was that what had called her almost five hundred miles across the desert? Steps down into the earth? She shut off the Lexus and listened to the engine tick as it cooled. The keys rattled on their ring as she pulled them out of the console, the gravel crunched under her feet as she walked up to the gate set in the chain link fence, and past it to the door of the metal-encased shed.

Up close, she could see the old wood, through the gaps in the metal sheets. Did something move there, in the dark? Did glittering eyes look back?

She fitted the key into the lock and found herself letting out a breath when it turned without difficulty, the padlock falling away, chains rattling against the door. The metal door had replaced the old wooden one, and she could tell, as she pushed it open, that the previous door had been bigger. To welcome in the faithful, right?

Inside, the place was dark and smelled like old dust, the stale smell of a crawlspace. The sky above was overcast, and in what little light filtered through the open door she could make out the backs of the nearest pews, festooned with cobwebs.

For a long time she stood on the threshold, imagining stepping through and being pelted from above by hundreds of spiders. When she was a little girl, still living in Atlanta, she had accidentally kicked a hole in the drywall of their shitty little apartment, and real-life brown recluses had come pouring out. Fiddlebacks, her mother had called them. Somehow, she had escaped with only a single bite, which had still necessitated a trip to the walk-in clinic that they couldn't afford, but the terror of that moment could still spike adrenaline into her system if she allowed herself to remember it too vividly.

A press of the rubbery button brought the flashlight she carried to life, carved out a cone of illumination from the shadowy interior of the shed. When it had been a church, Scott told her once, there had been a single window at each end, round, like the globe. But when his father covered it in metal, he covered the windows as well, and now no light could penetrate save that which fell in through the door she left hanging open behind her.

Inside, the church felt claustrophobic, the ceiling only a few feet above her head and seeming to hang dark and heavy there. The pews were lined up four deep on each side of the room, which was only a little bigger than a one-car garage. At the far end was what would have been an altar in some other church, but here seemed more like a lectern. The walls to either side held tacked-up pieces of paper that might once have borne mottos or slogans, but that had faded so much over time that they simply appeared blank, like mottled hide pinned to the walls. The only decoration that remained was an elaborately-carved wooden bas-relief on the far wall, depicting a map of the inner earth.

When Scott had told her about his grandfather's church, she had looked up the history of Hollow Earth theory. Atvatabar and Halley and John Cleves Symmes. This depiction looked like none of the maps that she had seen then. Not a hollow shell with a sun at the center, not a series of concentric globes within globes. This was more like a topographical map turned inside out, showing a seemingly infinite series of tunnels and chambers that ate into the earth like a cork.

As she moved closer, her light picking out details under the layers of dust, she could see cities that had been carved in some of the chambers, and great beasts that might have been Tobias Candish's dinosaurs. The carvings had been worn away by time and possibly by handling—had this been some holy relic, which the faithful touched for good luck?—and so what might once have been a detailed map of gleaming cities became ruins, festooned with cobwebs.

She walked between the pews and pressed her fingertips against the carving, which felt spongy beneath her hand, like wood that had been eaten up by termites. She had initially thought that the carving was hung on the wall, but as she got closer she saw that it *was* the wall, and it gave under her touch in a disquietingly fleshy manner. Then her hand went all the way through, into the hollow on the other side.

There was a second where she imagined the spiders. The fiddlebacks, hundreds of them scurrying across her fingertips, the flesh of her wrist and forearm. Her heart pounded in her ears and her vision swam with stars, but the spiders were only those of her imagination.

All she felt on the other side of the wall was the cool emptiness of a cave.

"My grandpa saw death as a set of stairs leading down into the dark," Scott told her once. "He said there was no entry point into the inner world at the North Pole or anyplace else. That in order to get there you had to leave your mortal body behind. He thought that there was room there for everyone who had ever died; that you would live in golden cities forever with the First People and the dinosaurs and everything else that had ever lived on the planet."

"What do you believe?" she had asked him. It had been early in their marriage still, and their relationship was filled with mysteries that hadn't yet been chased away by the dull light of routine.

"I don't believe in forever," he told her. "In anyplace or any thing that's free from entropy. Eternity without change is a wasteland. Nothing can live there."

When she had finished pushing her way through the strangely fungal carving at the back of the church, Leandra wasn't surprised to find herself at the top of a set of stone stairs.

The cave smelled like rock, cold and damp, and she could feel a current of air pressing up from below, buffeting against her skin.

Her flashlight was still on in her hand, but she didn't direct its beam down the steps. She just stood there, for a long time, feeling the cold cave air against her face, her hands, her shins. Then she turned around, went back between the pews, back out the door, and clicked the padlock behind her.

The inside of the house was mostly empty, the few pieces of furniture that remained making it feel like a dollhouse at a garage sale. There was an old recliner, covered in a heavy sheet. In the closet she found wire hangers that jangled when she touched them. In the kitchen was a heavy dining room table with no chairs, a bookshelf that had probably once served as a pantry, and an old refrigerator but only an empty space where a stove should have gone.

There was no food in the house, but the power was still on, so she drove down to the grocery store, walked up and down the aisles which seemed strangely shorter than the aisles at the grocery stores in the city, and then bought some bananas, a deli sandwich, some protein bars, and a box of Cheez-Its. She opened these and ate some of them in the car while she drove back to the house.

She put the food in the refrigerator, except for the box of Cheez-Its, which she carried around with her from room to room, leaving the occasional faint orange crumb behind. The house had only one floor, and Scott's bedroom was in the front, facing the road. It still held a bed and a nightstand, but no other furniture. She went and got the blanket out of the trunk of the car, and pulled the sheet off the recliner in the living room, then lay down on Scott's childhood bed and fell asleep.

In her dream, she was back in the tiny church. There was a strange violet glow coming from the mural at the back, and it limned the man who stood behind the lectern. His joints seemed overly large, his knuckles pronounced, but his skin was like paper over his bones, and the light seemed to shine through it, making him into a human lampshade.

Leandra had never met Scott's grandfather, but she knew, somehow, that this was him. His head was bald save for a few straggling white hairs, and he was preaching, gesticulating, spittle flying from his lips, but she couldn't hear him.

The pews were filled with parishioners who sat draped in white sheets like the one that had covered the recliner. Their silhouettes didn't appear fully human, somehow, and they moved beneath the sheets in strange, sudden jerks. They seemed like they had lost their shoulders, like they were holding their hands up to their chests, little children emulating a tyrannosaurus.

As she drew closer, she saw that the carving she had pushed her way through earlier in the day was gone, and in its place was something else. Something that shed the weird purple light. It was still a globe, and it was still hollow, but this one didn't look like a cork filled with beautiful cities gone to ruin. Instead, it showed that the crust of the earth was just a thin skin and beneath it there was nothing but a massive funnel web stretched taut, shining jet limbs uncurling in the darkness below.

Even as she realized that they really *were* uncurling, that it was not just some trick of the light but that the thing that she had taken as a carving was actually moving of its own volition, she shot awake in Scott's childhood bed. At the foot of it stood a man—she recognized him from the lectern of her dream, those rawboned hands, that skeletal frame—and at the same moment he was gone. Had disintegrated, it seemed, into a mass of tiny, crawling shadows which disappeared into every crack and crevice of the bedroom before her hand could find the switch.

The night air was cold this high up in the hills, and when Leandra stepped out the back door, her breath came in little clouds of fog. The flashlight was in her hand, the keys in the pocket of her slacks, a leather jacket—the only one she had thought to bring—wrapped tight against the chill.

When the light had come on in Scott's old bedroom, no sign of the man she had seen lingered, yet she had no doubt that she had seen *something*. A ghost, perhaps? The clinging remnants of whatever night terrors had once haunted Scott in this place, and still hung over him all these years later, so that he woke sweating and crying out in the darkness.

Scott had never given any indication that his relationship with his grandfather amounted to much, either good or bad, and yet Leandra knew how to read between the lines enough to know that Scott's fears and phobias were at least partially a shadow that the old man had cast. She had often wondered if Tobias Candish had done something to his grandson, when Scott was too young to consciously remember it. Or perhaps the fear was something that the grandfather had passed to the father, the father to his son?

There, in Scott's old bedroom, however, she had another thought. Perhaps Scott had *seen* something here that his young mind couldn't process. Something that he had subsequently...not *forgotten*, per se, but subsumed into his subconscious mind to such an extent that he couldn't put a name to it, couldn't tell anyone, not even her, the nature of his fear.

Had her husband seen a ghost, when he was still a child, sleeping in this room? But if the specter she had witnessed had been that of Tobias Candish, as she was somehow certain that it was, then who might Scott have seen at the foot of his bed, when his grandfather was still among the living?

These were the questions that had drawn her out into the chilly night, to the padlocked door of the old church. When she unlocked the metal door and pulled it open, she half expected to find the man from her dream standing in his accustomed place behind the lectern. The other half of her expected to shine her light on the unbroken bas-relief that made up the back wall, indicating that her earlier discovery of the tunnel behind it had been a hallucination brought on by suggestibility and grief.

Neither was the case. The church looked as it had when she left it hours before. No huddled parishioners, no violet light, no Tobias Candish—but the caved-in back wall remained, and the stone steps beyond it, leading down into the cold, cellar-smelling dark.

She should have called Godfrey. That much she knew. It's what a wise person would have done, before going into any unfamiliar place, cut off from the rest of the world, no one aware of where she was. She had read once, long ago, that an experienced caver never went spelunking alone, and never, ever without leaving details of their location with the outside world. Is that what she was doing, as she put her foot on the top of the stone steps? Was she going caving?

Her cell phone wasn't even in her jacket pocket. She had left it inside, on the bedside table in Scott's old room. If she didn't come back—if she disappeared like Scott had—then Godfrey would come looking for her. And, sooner or later, he would look here, just as she had. And he would find her phone.

What would that tell him? Would he look inside the shed, its door hanging open, the padlock dangling from its length of chain? And what would he find? An impossible passage leading down into the ground, or the back wall still intact, the bas-relief carving solid and unyielding?

She took the first step down and, even as she did, she knew that she wouldn't be coming back.

The steps were rough-hewn, but they had clearly been cut by hand. The walls and ceiling of the passage, likewise, were made of worked stone, which felt at odds with the wooden construction of the shed she was leaving behind. Was this something that Scott's grandfather had also built, or was it, instead, the reason why he had chosen this spot for his shed in the first place, built it around and atop some ruin that was already here?

Beneath her feet, the steps were damp but not slippery. Cellar-damp, not cave-damp, though she had never actually been in a cave in her life, only seen them on TV. This smelled like she imagined one would smell, though. Closed up and cold; the smell of minerals, of wet stone.

At first the steps went down straight enough, but after about twenty-five of them, she reached a landing where the stone steps turned to the right before continuing down into the dark. Except, Leandra realized as she turned, it *wasn't* dark, not any longer. Besides the illumination from the flashlight in her hand, the tunnel was lit by a cold, sourceless glow that reminded her of a blacklight.

By the time she reached the next landing, where the stairs once more turned at a right angle before continuing downward, she had shut off the flashlight entirely and stuck it into her jacket pocket. Here, beneath the earth, the air was actually warmer than it had been above, though still not comfortable. As her eyes searched her surroundings for the source of the light, which seemed to simply bleed impossibly from the stone itself, she noticed that the walls were home to faint bas-reliefs, worn nearly smooth by centuries of handling.

The style of them was reminiscent of carvings found in South and Central America, and they seemed to depict empires and battles, often against gargantuan shapes, all too faded to make out any details.

As she took the next step, and then the next, Leandra found herself struggling *not* to think about the walls around her—the impossibility of them. She was no archaeologist, but the stone was clearly ancient, even to her untrained eye, and the possibility that it had been here, buried beneath some shed in the backyard of a small house high in the hills outside Ogden was beyond unreasonable. Yet, the alternative was more unreasonable yet.

There was a part of her that was convinced that she was still asleep in Scott's bedroom. That maybe she was still asleep in her bed back home. That none of this had happened, and that she would wake up soon, having been infected temporarily by one of Scott's many nightmares. Or perhaps she would never wake up. Perhaps this was delusion, and she was sitting in some rest home somewhere, one paid for by the money in their shared accounts, overseen by Godfrey, still taking care of them even now that both of them were effectively gone.

More chilling than either of those scenarios was the fact that a part of her welcomed either of them. Better illusion and madness than a break from reality that was this complete.

"The work I do isn't really about deception," Scott used to say. "No one really thinks that I teleported from one place to another. That I sawed a woman in half. The trick isn't in fooling the audience who, in fact, came there to be fooled and are, as such, immune to it. No, the trick is the wonder. It's that moment between credulity and incredulity. It's not 'what did he do,' it's 'how did he do it.' If the audience thought for one minute that I had actually driven swords through someone, or transmuted a goldfish into a bouquet of flowers, they'd be terrified."

She should be terrified now, she knew. There was already a seed of it, somewhere deep in the back of her mind. A lizard-brain terror that told her that this was impossible. That this could not be, that it *must not be.* That warned her to turn and run, to never look back. To block this from her mind and never think of it again.

What kept her from it, most likely, was the grief. Like every other emotion, that primal fear was buried and muffled under an ache that rendered everything else into a distant echo. Nothing could penetrate that fog, not even the horror of the impossible tunnel that surrounded her, and so she kept descending.

By the time she reached the bottom, she had lost track of how many landings she had passed, how many times the stairs had turned and turned again. Their terminus was a low arch draped in vibrantly green lichen, beyond it a vista that should not have been shocking, given what she had already experienced, and yet still was. At the foot of the stairs, before the arch, was a short tunnel made of similar worked stone to that which she had already traversed. Beyond it, the cavern opened up into a soaring chamber, its dimensions organic, though it lacked many of the usual accoutrements of a natural cave.

In place of stalactites, stalagmites, or other cave formations, the cavern was populated by small structures reminiscent of the aboveground tombs in New Orleans which she and Scott had toured when he played that city.

Growing among them were things which gave the appearance of small trees, their branches denuded of leaves but draped with Spanish moss. Whether they were actually plants or some kind of odd, enormous fungus, Leandra couldn't guess—not anymore.

The graves themselves, if graves they were, were made from worked stone, and seemed newer than the passageway through which she had recently walked, though their true age was impossible to guess. Here and there, the sides were worked in bas-reliefs similar to those she had passed by, but less worn, so that she could make out shapes that seemed humanoid but moved on all fours, their arms or front limbs strangely elongated, their heads multi-faceted.

Sometimes, these figures were engaged in battle with other shapes, larger and stranger yet. Other times, they moved among domed structures unlike the tombs that now surrounded her. On at least one, she saw the hunched figures clustered around the base of a stepped pyramid, atop which stood a more human figure, a woman, who seemed to radiate a dark glow.

Where graves on the surface would have

been decorated with motifs of flowers, cherubs, or possibly skulls, these bore carvings of spiders and webs. Atop many of the crypts were reliefs of, presumably, their occupants. Like the figures on the sides, these were at once human and strangely not, their features somehow muted by the technique which depicted them. Here and there, crypts had also been broken open, the tops lying shattered on the ground beside them, the interiors shadowy dark and empty, save for the copious cobwebs that had settled there.

As she passed among them, Leandra had the strange urge to break one of the tombs open, to see what was inside. Were there bodies in them? Or something else, something waiting to be born, rather than something dead?

The whole chamber felt like a studio backlot to her as she walked through it. The impossible trees, the hanging moss, a low fog that clung to her ankles, the tombs thrown together by a set dresser working on a budget and a deadline. None of it could be here, and it had that unmistakable staginess that came with tableaux that were built where they should not be.

At the same time, she had no doubts as to

the reality of it all. She could smell the cavern in which she stood, the scent of damp stone mixed now with loamy earth. She could feel the humidity of the place on her skin. When she let her fingertips rest on one of the tomblike structures, it had the solidity of real stone.

There was something else, too. Now and then, she caught movement out of the corner of her eye. A subtle scuttling motion, nothing she could ever assign a cause to before it was gone behind the next tomb, the next stunted tree. Something large, though, she knew. As large as she was, sometimes bigger. Figures, dark and hunched, moving in the shadows of the cave. Keeping pace with her. Watching her.

The cavern itself was longer than it was tall, and at its far end was another archway, this one larger than the one she had entered. Its keystone was decorated with a sigil of some sort, daubed on with a dark paint that looked suggestively like blood. The symbol was of a circle, partially bisected from above by a single, straight line.

Leandra's attention didn't remain on the arch for very long, however. Instead, as she approached, she was immediately arrested by the three figures which stood below it, clearly waiting for her. All three were familiar, in their way, though she had never precisely seen any of them before. The one farthest to the right was Tobias Candish, as he had appeared in her dream, as he had appeared at the foot of Scott's bed.

He wore a suit with a bolo tie, though both were slightly disheveled, and his skin seemed paper-thin, as it had in the dream. He still looked mostly human, but it was as if his bones were the wrong size and shape beneath a human suit, lending him an uncanny air of mutability, as though something was about to change.

Next to him stood a figure wearing the suit that they had buried Scott's father in. Leandra had never known Michael Candish particularly well, and even if she had, she wouldn't be able to recognize him now. Only the top part of his face and hair remained, like an empty mask that had been pushed up his head by the splitting of his jawbone into two mandibles which opened to the side, like the chelicerae of a spider. No eyes watched her from the eyeholes in that empty mask.

Instead, a cluster of green, jewel-like glim-
mers peered out from beneath it.

On the far left hunched the figure that
Leandra would have recognized most immediately. Not from his features, for they were
hidden by his posture and the position of his
arms, but from the way he flinched away from
his surroundings. She wanted to run to Scott,
and it wasn't the strangeness of the situation
that stopped her, but the fact that she knew
when Scott was in such distress, it wasn't wise
to approach him too abruptly.

Where the other two figures stood straight,
Scott was crouched, his arms up in front of
his face, as though warding himself against a
blow. He still wore the tuxedo he had worn
into the coffin, and it was smeared with dirt
and grime. His hands, too, seemed to be
stained black, where he clawed them into fists
above his head.

"Scott," she said, approaching slowly, keeping her voice quiet and level.

"Stay back," Scott's voice said, but it didn't
come from the crouched figure that she knew
was him. It came from the lips of the wizened
cadaver that was his grandfather.

"You know that she can't," another voice

said, this one from the moving mouthparts of
the thing that wore the suit Michael Candish
had been buried in. It wasn't Scott's father's
voice, however. It sounded a little like a pho-
nograph recording, scratchy and harsh, and
though she hadn't been able to hear him in
her dream, she knew that it was the voice of
Tobias Candish.

"We thought it was you, but it always had
to be her." It had been years since Leandra
had heard Michael Candish speak, but she
knew that the third voice belonged to him,
even as it issued from the crouched figure of
his son. Like the voice of Tobias, it was tinny
and strangely mechanical sounding.

"You know she has to come with us," Tobias's voice again. "That's why you're here."

Leandra had stopped when they began talking, but now she started to move again, inch-
ing forward slowly, approaching Scott with
one hand outstretched. She said his name
again, then, "Look at me."

The arms lowered from his face. Even in the
dim light of the cavern, she could see how
he had changed. His eyes, which had always
been a bottomless hazel with green flecks,
were now onyx black from edge to edge. His

skin looked gray and sunken, and a black seam split his chin from his lip to somewhere beneath the collar of his tuxedo.

"Lee," he said, and it was beyond disconcerting to see the recognition light even these transformed eyes, and yet hear his voice issue from somewhere off to the right.

Had she still possessed any doubts that she had found him, that would have dispelled them. He was the only one who had called her Lee since her Nana died.

"Scott," she said, and walked to him. For a moment he reached out his blackened hands to her, then he saw them and drew them back.

"Things have changed, Lee," he said, from the lips of his grandfather.

"They don't have to," she offered, but even as she said it, she knew how ridiculous it was.

"They do," the voice of Michael Candish said.

"It's like I used to say," Scott's voice again. "Nothing lasts forever, not even forever."

"What is this place?" Leandra asked.

This time, the three voices spoke in unison, though they all said different things. "The grave," said Scott. "The stars," said his father. "Eternity," said Tobias Candish.

"I don't understand," Leandra said.

"We shouldn't stay here," Scott's voice replied.

"Follow us, if you will," Tobias said. "We'll walk and talk."

What else was there to do, there in that impossible place, deep beneath the surface of the world, in a cavern that could not exist, talking to two men who had been dead for years, and to her husband, who had been missing for more than a month? She followed them.

"First there were great beasts, titans, giants in the earth." It was the voice of Tobias Candish that did most of the speaking, though it seemed to jump from body to body. "And before them, perhaps, something else. Who knows? Then came the First People, the Golden People. They threw down the giants and built an ageless empire, eternal. But decay exists in all things, even eternity, and the seeds of their dissolution had already been sown.

"When I preached of golden cities and eternal paradise, I didn't yet understand this fundamental truth. I saw into the earth not as it is, but as it was. And yet, it was as it is, and it is as it was. All things are the same, even as they change."

"I don't know what that means," Leandra said.

"When you sleep," this was Michael's voice, "do you sometimes dream of being a little girl again? Or in high school? Of when you and Scott first met?"

"Of course."

"Then who are you in the dream? Are you the person you are now, or the person you were then? When you wake up, you are in the present moment, but when you dream, you are in the past, or the future, or some moment that has never existed. That is what it's like here."

"We walk in the ruins of those golden cities now," Tobias's voice again. "But once, they were here and shining, and in the future, perhaps they will be so again. For now, this is what we are. Scuttling shadows, waiting for our turn at the light. And it is coming, even as it is doomed to end. The stories have been carved here since before they began, before there was anyone here to carve them."

"What does this have to do with me?" Leandra asked. "With Scott."

"When I was a young man, I began having dreams," Tobias Candish's voice said. "They showed me the interior of the earth, the past that I thought was the future and might yet be. I started the church, and I tried to preach the gospel, but I knew, even then, that I had been shown the truth for some other reason. There was something waiting for me on the other side. I thought perhaps it would be my son, and then, I thought it would be Scott."

"I saw something," Scott's voice spoke, from his father's mandibles. "When I was little. Dad had warned me never to go into the shed already, but I didn't listen. I saw things before that, too. Trap doors in the ground that weren't there. Eyes watching me in the dark.

"I went into the church, and I sat down in one of the pews. The back wall was gone, like it had never been there. The church was just a tube, with darkness at one end, and in that darkness, they were waiting for me. Thousands of them. Millions. Everyone who had ever died. Maybe more than that.

"They were waiting for a leader, someone who could unite them, the way that their predecessors had been united. Someone who could prepare them for what was to come. Grandpa thought it was me. Dad was afraid that it was me. But it was always you, Lee. It was always you."

"Scott saw more clearly than I ever did," Tobias spoke again. "I understand that now. At the time, though, it was all so confusing, and he didn't know what had happened. He saw only the masses that waited for him below, all clambering to reach him and, through him, you. I had been shown the way so that I could show it to him, so that someday he could leave behind a trail of breadcrumbs that would lead you to us."

They walked as they spoke, through the crumbling ruins of a once-great city. The buildings around her called to mind pictures she had seen in a book of Angkor Wat, though she had never been, not even when Scott had played Bangkok. They must once have been magnificent, but now they were crumbling. The roofs of many had fallen in, and the stone walls were streaked with grime, and festooned with webs. It reminded her of the old English gothic movies that her mom used to watch on afternoon TV, the way that the set decorators always seemed to go overboard with the fake cobwebs.

Down the alleys and the byways, Leandra could see movement. Huge shapes, much bigger than those that accompanied her, shifting in the dim distance, passing stealthily between buildings, despite their size. Reminders that not everything down here was a person, or ever had been.

"But why me?" Leandra asked. There was more to the question that she didn't speak aloud, and yet she thought that, somehow, Scott heard it. *I'm nobody*, the question said. *I've never been anybody. I'm just Scott's shadow. That's all I've ever wanted to be.*

The body of Tobias Candish shrugged its shoulders, though his voice spoke from the splitting lips of his grandson. "Why anybody? Why anything? It has always been you."

Their walk took them to the steps of a broken-down temple. Its skyline—if such a word could even be applied in this place—had once been a mass of domes piled atop domes. Now, it lay buried beneath a snowfall of cobwebs and decay.

"They're waiting inside," Michael's voice said.

"Who?"

"Your subjects. Your people. Your flock."

"What are they waiting for?"

"They're waiting for you."

The inside of the temple was as much a ruin as the outside had been. And as out there, impossibly huge shadows sometimes moved in the recesses, occupying rooms into which they should not have been able to squeeze. Yet, these shapes never molested them, and Scott and his forebears led them unerringly to the center of the complex, where a set of stone stairs cut a spiral even deeper into the earth.

Down and down and down they went, and Leandra knew that her lungs should be burning, her legs aching and rubbery. But perhaps there was something to be said for having an eternal body, even one that wouldn't last forever.

"I used to think that I didn't believe there was anything waiting for us after we died," Scott said quietly, as they walked down the stairs. His voice, for once, settling in his own body for the moment. "I thought there was nothing. Just blackness. 'I had been dead for billions and billions of years before I was

born, and had not suffered the slightest in-
convenience from it.' Now I know, though. I
didn't really *think* there was nothing. I prayed
that there was."

She tried to take his blackened hand, there
on the stairs, but he pulled it self-consciously
away, and she didn't push, because she knew
not to.

The experience of reaching the bottom of
the twisting stairs was disorienting. She felt
like she was still moving, even as she stopped,
the dreamlike sensation of drifting, like when
you lie down in bed after having been in a
boat, and you can still feel yourself floating.

That the room at the base of the stairs was
impossible should have come as no surprise
to her by now. That it was a throne room,
perhaps no more so. Yet both did catch her
off guard. The room itself was hexagonal,
though of such massive proportions as to
make the identification of its shape no easy
task. It stretched up and up, its ceiling lost in
the haze of blue-black light which filled it, as
it had all the rest of the underground world.

Here were the subjects of which the others
had spoken. The flock. They numbered in the
hundreds, perhaps even the thousands, and

yet she knew that this was only the merest fraction of them. "Everyone who had ever died," that's what Scott had said his grandfather believed was in the Hollow Earth, what Tobias Candish said that his grandson had seen waiting for her.

Here they were, if it was them indeed. They scuttled and crept and hunched and crawled. Some were nearly human, their skin turned gray or pale, creases splitting their bottom jaws. Others had shed every vestige of their former humanity, could be identified only by scraps of funeral clothes that still clung to them here and there. The cuffs of a tuxedo. The tatters of a burial shroud.

All of them seemed to be caught somewhere on a spectrum between human and spider, and looking across their sea of faces, of mandibles, of multitudinous eyes, Leandra experienced a moment's horror, the last, lingering flicker of the fear she had felt when she kicked open the wall of her apartment and was buried in brown recluses. She didn't have her husband's phobia, however. She couldn't have. She had spent too many nights in the dark with him, holding his hand through the terrors. She had to be able to look into them without flinching.

Now she did just that, and as she walked across the massive room, the multitudes ceased their scuttling movement, and bowed as she passed. In the center of the chamber was a step pyramid that seemed to be so tall it could have no summit, and yet it did, and atop it was a throne that looked like it had been cut from a basalt statue. What did the statue depict? Was it a spider, or a many-armed human figure? Perhaps it was something else entirely, or had been something once, and had been reconsecrated time and again—a bat turned to a spider turned to a goddess turned to what?

As she ascended the pyramid, the three ghosts who had led her here kept pace. Michael Candish walked on one side of her, Tobias behind, and Scott on her other side. At the top of the steps, she turned and looked out across the crowd that surrounded her.

This must be what Scott saw, on the stage, after he had performed his best illusion, when he stepped out to absorb the adulation and applause of the audience. This moment of being the sun, shining down on everyone else. But no sun could shine this far below the earth. If she was to be a star, she would have to be a darker one.

Without another word from her guides, Leandra took her place on the throne. The stone beneath her was cold and hard, but it fit her, as if it had been made for her frame. In front of her now, Tobias turned out to face the crowd that surrounded them, and dropped to one knee. From behind him, she could see how flimsy his human disguise truly was. There was so little left of the man he had been on the surface.

Michael Candish took a position on one side of her throne, Scott on the other. "What is to become of me now?" Scott said quietly, his voice barely a whisper, not meant for anyone to hear, probably not even her.

"I don't know," she said to him, in the same voice that she had used to soothe him when his nightmares had awakened them both in the dark. "No one knows, because not even eternity can last forever. But as long as I am here, there will be a place for you beside me."

She did not reach for Scott's hand, but instead simply extended her own. After a moment's hesitation, he took it.

HOLLOW EARTHS

A single bat lands with a thud on a mountain of guano. Its wings beat at the mound, but they cannot carry it aloft again, for it is too weighted down by the mass of its own excretions. From out of the mountain come cockroaches—first one or two questing antennae, then dozens, hundreds, swarming up from the digested remains of the bat's former prey—they mass over the body of the bat, which thrashes and squeaks in its impotent rage and terror, and bit by bit they tear it apart. Pale crabs join them in their feasting, boxy bodies looming over the low carapaces of the roaches, pulling off bits of bat flesh with their pincers. Eventually, nothing remains but a skeleton and, over time, it too disappears into the mound. So, we see how a king may go a progress through the guts of a beggar.

From the Deposition of Annabel Chambers

Q: When did you last see Miss Martin?

A: You mean Dom?

Q: Dominique Martin, yes. When was the last time you were in contact?

A: I hadn't seen her in years. Before the other day, I mean. We used to be friends, back in small times...

Q: Small times?

A: Since we were both little kids. We lived in the same apartments. She was across the parking lot from me. So we were in different buildings, but our bedrooms were maybe a hundred feet apart. You just went out our door, down the steps, past the cars, across the parking lot, up the stairs, and you were knocking on Dom's door.

Q: And you were friends?

A: I mean, yeah. Best friends, I guess, back when we were kids and we believed in stuff like best friends, y'know?

Q: But you said you hadn't seen her in years.

A: Right. The apartments caught on fire when we were in junior high, I guess. Eighth grade. My building burned down completely, Dom's not all the way but enough, y'know?

Sparks blew over from my side onto their roof. That's what the firemen told us. We lost everything in the fire, my mom and me. We moved after that. Changed towns, changed schools. Mom said she wanted to get away, get a new start. Which meant that I lost Dom, too.

Q: And you didn't try to stay in touch at all?

A: We were kids, and this was a few years ago. It wasn't all smartphones and Facebook and shit yet, though, I mean, that was right around the corner. I went to high school, I guess Dom did too, and we just...lost track, y'know?

Q: Until Miss Martin contacted you on... April 17th?

A: Sure, if that's what I said before. I don't remember for sure, but it was through Facebook, so there'd be a record, I guess.

Q: What'd she say?

A: She said she wanted to get together. We'd both graduated, were both out on our own now. She said she missed me, wanted to catch up. All the usual stuff. She said she was still in town, and my mom had moved back, so I had a good excuse to drive in, meet Dom.

Q: And you met her…four days ago, is that correct? On Thursday, April 30th?

A: If that's the date. But yeah, I guess it was four days ago. That's what they tell me.

Q: Where did you meet?

A: This coffee shop. By the community college. I forget the name of it now. Something with Leaf in the name, I think.

Q: The New Branch Coffee House, on Perimeter Drive.

A: Branch, yeah, that's it.

Q: So what did you talk about?

A: The usual stuff. Small times, the old days. Our jobs. Dom looked different, but then, the last time I'd seen her she'd been, what, fourteen?

Q: Different how?

A: She'd gained a little weight, I guess, and she'd put a purple streak in her hair. She dressed different now than when she was fourteen, who doesn't?

Q: Did she look like she was in trouble? Like she was on drugs?

A: The fuck does that mean? What does someone who's *in trouble* look like?

Q: All I'm asking is, did anything seem wrong?

A: Well, no, not at first. She seemed like maybe she wasn't sleeping a lot, but she said she was taking college classes on the side, so, y'know, that would account for it, right?

Q: You said, "not at first."

A: Right. I mean, obviously, something was wrong, wasn't it? I'm fucking sitting here now, aren't I?

Q: Did you realize something was wrong while you were at the coffee shop?

A: I...don't know, really. I mean, now, sitting here, I think I did, but did I think so then, or am I just making it up? Hindsight, and all that. I know I was happy to see Dom again, happier than I'd expected to be. And I felt guilty.

Q: Guilty?

A:For not, y'know, being there for her. Trying to get in touch sooner. It'd been, shit, another thirteen, fourteen years since the fire. I could've tried to look her up once the internet really became a thing, y'know? Found her once Facebook took off.

Q: The way she found you?

A: Yeah. So things fell right back into the old rhythms, we were making the same old jokes, talking about the same stuff, and it was like no time had passed at all, except that I was feeling guilty, and that's when she brought up the Game.

Q: The game?

A: Yeah. That's where it all went to shit, isn't it?

When we were kids, we used to play this game. I mean, little kids have obsessions, right? Princesses, ponies, fire trucks, whatever movie they watch over and over again right that minute. (I suppose so. Go on.) Well, with Dom it was always the same thing, all the way from small times. She was really into Hollow Earth stuff.

(Hollow earth stuff?)

Right. So, I dunno, back in the 1800s or whenever, there were all these theories that the world was hollow, instead of solid. Like, you know how in school they teach you that the world is made up of layers of dirt and then rock and then lava or something, and at the center there's this really dense core spinning around, keeping all the electromagnetism flowing or whatever? There was that movie where they had to jumpstart it with a nuke. Did you ever see that?

(No, I can't say that I did.)

It was dumb as balls. Anyway, that's what you learn in school, but we didn't *always* know that, right? So before we figured all that shit out, there were guys who were convinced that the earth was hollow and filled with… other worlds, I guess, on the inside. Guys named Symmes and Haley and shit like that. They tried to raise money to organize expeditions to the North Pole cuz they thought that's where they'd find a way in. Some of them started churches. All sorts of crazy stuff.

(Crazy stuff?)

I just mean…these guys really believed in all this, y'know? And Dom was really into it all. She had books these guys had written, and maps and charts and stuff taped up on her bedroom wall. Drawings of what these guys thought the Hollow Earth looked like, because of course they didn't all agree. Some of them thought it was just like a big hollow globe, with a tiny sun in the center; and others thought that it was a bunch of globes within globes—what do they call that? concentric!—and that each, I dunno, *layer* I guess rotated separately from the others. Hell, some of them even thought we were *already* inside the Hollow Earth; that when we looked up at the sky and the stars we were actually just looking *in*. That's pretty dumb, but maybe it's also a good metaphor.

(We're not here for metaphors.)

In that case, I think you're probably going to be disappointed with my story.

(That's as may be, but why don't you tell me anyway. Tell me about the game.)

Okay, well, when we were little kids, we played pretend, right, like little kids do. Only Dom pretty much always wanted to play Hollow Earth stuff. The way it started out was that she'd pick a door and we would pretend that when we opened it, instead of the laundry room or her closet or my mom's bedroom we'd find a set of stone stairs leading down, and we'd follow them into the Hollow Earth. Or we'd go out exploring in the neighborhood and we'd look for tunnels leading down—storm drains, drainage ditches—anything that went down into the ground, and we'd go down into them to see if they led to the Hollow Earth.

I mean, I guess most kids are kinda obsessed with those things, right? They feel sort of forbidden and scary. Trolls live there, or whatever. Monsters. Except with Dom it was spiders.

(Spiders?)

Well, kind of, but I'm getting ahead of myself. If I'm gonna try to explain this, I gotta try to do it in order, or it'll make even *less* sense. So, Dom was all into these old Hollow Earth theories, but she also thought they were all wrong. She had her own instead. When we were little I guess I just thought it was a made-up story, or something that she got from one of her books. Dom's Hollow Earth wasn't an empty globe, it was more like a... like a hive. Like underneath the world was just caves, cave after cave, all carved out until the earth was all full of holes, like a piece of cork. And all those caves led to caverns, and the caverns were filled with cities and lakes and forests. Giant mushrooms sometimes, but weird plants, too, that lived off the light from the caves. Luminous rocks and all sorts of weird stuff, enough to make there be day and night, even though you were miles underground. Because the Hollow Earth was kind of magic, I guess. I dunno, it wasn't my story, it was Dom's.

However it all worked, she had this whole

history for it. The Hollow Earth was older than the regular earth, according to her. There were people down there before the dinosaurs came, this "first race" of "golden people" who built huge cities with towers and temples and whatnot. She said that the cities down there looked kind of like the ones in Cambodia and kind of like the ones in Central America and kind of like...well, you get the point. The people who lived on the surface of the world—that's us—we were descended from these golden people, but the golden people were still down there, too, at least for a long time. And there were dinosaurs, like in an Edgar Rice Burroughs book.

(Who?)

He wrote Tarzan, but he also wrote these books about the Hollow Earth—like I said, it was all the rage back then. He called his Pellucid-something, I think. Anyway, in Dom's version of things there were dinosaurs down there way after they had died out up here, and the golden people lived alongside them, mostly in harmony, because even though the Hollow Earth was a real, physical place, it was also kind of like heaven. When you went there, you lived forever.

So, when we played the Game, as kids, we would pretend to go down into the Hollow Earth, and the golden people would recognize us as their descendants, and we would be royalty, of course, and they would crown us queens and we would ride dinosaurs and fight monsters and...y'know, all that little kid stuff. But there was another part to it, especially as we got older.

I already said we'd go exploring, looking for tunnels and whatever, but we also just went looking for doors. Dom would try to find a door she had never opened before, and before she opened it she would kind of hold her breath, and at the time I thought it was part of the Game but now, I think maybe she really was hoping that when she opened it up it might really, finally be the door that actually led to those stone steps that went down and down and down. She was obsessed with it, more and more as we got older. She'd jimmy open locked doors at school, break into abandoned buildings, go exploring in places plastered with *No Trespassing* signs.

(And when you met at the coffee shop, she wanted to play the game again?)

Right, but this time she had a specific door

in mind. She said she'd been back to the apartments, now that she was living in town again. I had driven by them myself, on my way to the coffee shop, and I had seen that they never got fixed up. Mine was all bull-dozed down now, nothing left, the rubble all carted up and hauled away, but the one that Dom had lived in still had the first floor walls intact, just nothing on the inside. An empty space. Hollow.

(Yes, go on.)

What? Sorry. Dom said she'd been back, that the basement was still there, and that there was a door in it now that hadn't been there before. She wanted to go open it.

(Basement?)

Yeah, there was a basement. Not under my building but under Dom's. It had the laun-dromat for both buildings in it, but it also had a storm shelter. In case of tornadoes, y'know? That's where Dom said the door was.

(And you went with her?)

… I did, yeah.

(But you didn't want to?)

I don't know. I mean, it seemed crazy. Still does, really. And I couldn't imagine that the place was safe, after all these years. Maybe it

was full of, I dunno, poison mold or asbes-
tos or something. Maybe that was why they
hadn't rebuilt it. But I also thought... I was
guilty, like I said, and I thought maybe Dom
was just suggesting this because it's something that we did when we were kids. Maybe
she just wanted to reconnect. So yeah, I had
my fucking reservations, but I went with her.

(So, the two of you went back to the apartment complex where you grew up?)

Yeah. We took my car, because Dom said
she had taken the bus to the college and then
walked to the coffee shop. We stopped by a
gas station on the way and she bought some
candy bars. "For sustenance," she said. You
can probably verify that with her credit card
company, or something, right? Anyway, I figured she was just hungry and wanted some
candy, or that it was all part of play-acting
the "adventuring party" and heading down
into the dark dungeon or whatever. She stuck
those in her bag and we drove over and parked
near the apartment buildings.

It was afternoon by then, overcast and
spooky. The walls all still standing up, the
top edges blackened to charcoal, the windows
empty, no glass or nothing. No doors. They

had cleared out the inside, so that it wasn't as dangerous if kids came and trespassed, which is what we had to do, because there was a chain link fence around the whole place now. We didn't have to climb over, though. There was a place already, one that Dom went right to. You've probably found it by now. Where you could pull the fence up and kinda skootch under. We went through there, and then into what used to be Dom's building.

I'm sorry, I know I'm getting a little choked up here, which probably seems weird.

(Take your time. Just tell it however you need to tell it.)

It's just that…I could still remember right where everything had been, y'know? I was standing in this empty spot, where the ground was all black and gritty from where they had bulldozed everything except the walls, and I knew the moment I stepped over what would have been the threshold of Dom's room, even though it was three stories above my head back in the old days.

Back then there was a door that led to the stairs leading down to the laundry room, and also an elevator, but they had filled the shaft up with big chunks of broken-up concrete and rock. The stairs were still there, though, just with no door now, and a pool of rainwater down at the foot of them, where they turned a corner and then there was a metal door with a padlock sorta *draped* across it, but not locked, not anymore.

(Because Miss Martin had unlocked it?)

I don't know. But yeah, that's what I thought, when I saw it, was of her picking locks when we were kids.

She took the chain off, wrapped it around the handle of the door, and then pushed the door open. It was dark on the other side, but not completely dark. The laundry room ceiling was concrete too, part of the foundation of the building, but during the fire it had been weakened or damaged or something and now there were holes in it. Up above, they had laid in metal grates to cover them up, but the grates let in light, at least a little, and also water, so that the floor of the laundry room was probably an inch deep with rain water. When I stepped in I could feel it, sloshing around my Doc Martens. I was worried about snakes and god-knows-what. I wanted to go back, but Dom was already going ahead of me.

They hadn't taken out the laundry machines, I don't know why. They were still lined up there, in two rows, facing each other. Washers on one side and dryers on the other. We had to walk between them. I'm not a little kid anymore, but I've seen dumb horror movies, and I was picturing arms reaching out of those black openings and grabbing my legs the whole fucking way, you bet I was...

(You stopped talking. What happened next?)

I don't want to tell you what happened next.

(Does that really seem like an option, at this point?)

No...it's just...okay, so, I know that what I'm about to say is fucking crazy, all right. I know that. And I know that I'm going to be telling it to whatever you cops have that passes for a shrink here in another day or two, but whatever. Whatever. I'll tell you, too. Why not? What choice do I have? I guess I could make something up, though that's what you and the shrink and everyone else maybe me included will say I'm doing anyway, but... okay, here goes:

We walked through the laundry room and

pushed open the door to the storm shelter. Back when we were kids, the storm shelter had a foosball table and some other stuff in it, but that was all gone now. It was just an empty, dirty, dark room. Dom took a flashlight out of her bag—something bright, a bike headlight I think—and it lit up the room. And…

You remember I said that when I walked into the place where the building used to be, it was like I had never left? I could remember exactly where Dom's room had been, could count the steps in my head up to her apartment? Well, I remembered the storm shelter, too. It had been just a square, concrete room. That's it. One door in, the one we just walked through. No other door out. Now, though, there was another door on the far side of the room.

If you go back there—if you haven't already—I don't know if you'll find it there or not, but it was there then, just like Dom had said it was. The door wasn't metal, like the one leading to the laundry room or the one from the laundry room to here. It was wood, and it looked old, which made even less sense than it suddenly being there where no door had ever been before.

A symbol had been painted on it in something black that still felt tacky under my fingertips. A circle, with a long, straight line piercing it from above, like what the utility guys paint on the sidewalks and lawns in my mom's new neighborhood to mark the location of buried lines. The door didn't have a knob, it had a handle, and Dom smiled back at me before she pushed it down and then pushed it open, holding her breath like she did when we were kids…

(And? What was on the other side of the door? Annabel, I'm going to need you to talk to me…)

Right, sorry. First, though, I guess I should tell you about the spiders.

(Okay, if that's what you feel like you need to do.)

So…I said that when we were kids, Dom had this whole history of the Hollow Earth, right, and how it was eternal and when you went down there you lived forever. Well, as we got older, the story started to change. See, before the golden people, there were apparently other things that lived down there. Giant monsters, shit like Godzilla and Gamera and whatever. Titans, she called them, like in Greek mythology. And, like in Greek mythology, the golden people had thrown the Titans down.

Before that the golden people were simple, tribal, sort of like cavemen. They were nomadic, traveling around from one cavern to another. It was conquering the Titans that gave them civilization. They had to band together to beat them, and that was a start, but there was more to it than that. The Titans couldn't die, so the golden people imprisoned them someplace in the center of the center of the world, and it was on their shoulders that the golden people built their great cities. Like…once the Titans were imprisoned, they became a power source, like a battery. Don't ask me how any of this works, because it was Dom's fairy tale, not mine. But even in a fairy tale, you can't just do something like that and not pay the price.

(The price?)

Dom said it was like radioactivity. We get nuclear power, right, but the tradeoff is that it's radioactive, dangerous, it gets into everything, sooner or later, poisons the planet. We get energy from coal, but to do that we have to burn it, and that puts smoke into the air, eventually it'll choke us all to death. Whatever we do to drive our world, there's a tradeoff, right? So, when the golden people threw down the Titans and used them for energy, they built these incredible marvels, but gradually the people and their cities rotted from the inside out.

They were still eternal, though. They didn't die or fade away like Tolkien's elves, they just…changed. Into these things partway between people and spiders—don't ask me why, I asked Dom once and she just replied, with the characteristic logic of a kid, that it was just how it was. These spider-people—Dom called them ghouls—built a new empire in the ruins of the old. They fed on the dead and the dying and waited for their time to come up and seize the world of light and life. These are Dom's words now, I'm just parroting them back to you.

(You'll pardon my saying so, but that sounds a lot less appealing than magic cities filled with dinosaurs.)

Yeah, but Dom was still convinced that we wanted to go. That the Hollow Earth was still something more than all this, y'know?

(You think this hollow earth was someplace where she was special?)

No. I mean, yeah, when we were little that was it. We weren't very popular in school, and I think we were both lonely kids…I think… I think maybe we're both just lonely bigger kids now. But it wasn't just a way to feel special. There was more to it. It was…it was a way for the *world* to feel special, y'know? A way to believe that there was something more than four walls. More than just going in to work every day. Not more *for us*, necessarily, just more at all. Like…did you ever play that game Bloody Mary?

(I may have, but you tell me about it.)

So you look in the mirror and you say *Bloody Mary, Bloody Mary, Bloody Mary* or whatever. Maybe you say it three times or five or something, I can't remember. It was in that movie *Candyman* too, right, so maybe you say *Candyman* instead. Whatever you say, you stand, and you look in the mirror, and you say it, and then she appears, or he does, and they kill you. So why the hell would you ever do that? To prove to your friends that you're brave? To prove to *yourself* that you are? That's a fucking dumb reason to risk getting

killed, right? So maybe you do it because…
because it would be *worth it*, if you got killed.
If Candyman appeared over your shoulder or
Bloody Mary reached out her bloody hands
from behind the glass, because then, just as
you died, at least you'd *know* that there was
something magical in the world, even if it was
also terrible.

(Do you think that's what Miss Martin
wanted when she opened that door? To die?)

I don't know what Dom wanted. I really don't. And if I thought I did, before she
opened that door, then I sure as hell don't
now. I don't even know what I wanted, but
I know what I expected to see. Not a god-
damn thing. I expected the door to open onto
a concrete wall, or onto dirt, because there
was no place else for it to go, not from there.

(And what did you see?)

Steps, of course. Stone steps, leading down
into the dark…

**From notes left behind by Annabel Cham-
bers, written on white legal paper**

Mom just left. She begged me to tell the
police what really happened. I guess it's been
long enough now that they've figured out that

Dom isn't coming back. I guess they've decided that she's dead. Maybe they've decided that I killed her.

The police shrink, Dr. Schriver, says that I'm not being held, because there's insufficient evidence, but she also told me that I'm not supposed to leave town, so…I don't know what you call that. House arrest, maybe, here in the guest room of my mom's new house, that hasn't ever been home to me.

Dr. Schriver comes by once a week. She says that I'm supposed to write this stuff down, like I'm writing now. She says it's for me, to help me remember, to help me "process," but she collects the pages whenever I'm done, so hi there, Dr. Schriver.

You say you don't think that I had anything to do with Dom's disappearance, but you also say you think I know more than I'm telling. You say that right now my mind is "protecting me from the truth," but that if I really work with you, I'll be able to remember what actually happened. You should probably talk to my mom. Between the two of you, I'll bet you could work out a story that you'd like better. I can't. All I've got is what I remember, and what I remember is this:

Dom opens the door and there are the steps. They're stone and they're old, much older than the burned-up apartment building, much older than the storm shelter with its damp concrete. These are Mayan ruin steps, Pyramids at Giza steps.

They go down into the dark, but the dark isn't dark. When we start down, Dom shuts off the flashlight, and we can still see. There's a light that isn't light. It comes from things that grow on the walls of the cavern, from luminous strata in the rock itself. In school, when we went to the museum, there was this room that had a black curtain over the door and when you stepped inside there were rocks in a case. You pushed a button and a black light came on and suddenly the rocks glowed these marvelous fluorescent colors. The rocks in the cave do that, too, but they do it on their own, no need for a button.

We go down, and sometimes the tunnel is natural, sometimes it's man-made—or *something*-made—but always the steps, and as we go, I can tell that we're going deeper and deeper, toward the heart of the world. We're going down into Dom's Hollow Earth, and I wonder, as we travel, if we're going to the one filled with golden people and dinosaurs, or the one filled with cobwebs and rot and giant spiders, and I wonder if Dom cares all that much, one way or the other.

She's walking ahead of me. Excited, a kid again, lacking even the motes of trepidation that I still carry. She practically skips down the steps, weightless down here in the dark heart of the world, where she has always belonged.

We come out into a cavern, and it's all glowing fungi. Mushrooms as tall as redwoods shedding purple and blue light down onto us both. Things move among the mushrooms, big shapes, too big to be Dom's ghouls, but definitely relatives somehow. I see one of them pass between the stalks, its body like a spider's but without enough legs. Bones make up its outside, but something is alive inside them. A dinosaur skeleton in the museum that got up and took a walk, but underneath living black carapace and glittering eyes, cobwebs making tendons and muscles, making the great jaws hinge open and closed.

It doesn't come after us, maybe because it isn't interested, maybe because Dom is there, and it knows, somehow, that she belongs.

Beyond that cavern is another tunnel, more steps, then another cavern, a city all in ruins. The buildings have fallen in on themselves, their domes and towers pitted like an apple eaten through by worms.

You'll like this part, Dr. Schriver. I've been having a dream, lately, ever since Dom disappeared, and at this point I can't tell if the dream is a memory or just a dream. In it, we're in that ruined city, except Dom isn't there, I'm by myself, and I hear this voice, lifted in a kind of singsong chant. *The worms crawl in, the worms crawl out,* it sings. *The worms play pinochle on your snout.* Funny, that's the only thing I know about pinochle.

I follow the sound, and there's a man standing there. Or, at least, something that looks like a man. He's wearing a suit and tie, not quite a tuxedo, but almost. Like he's dressed up for prom or something. But his head is hanging down, he's looking at his hands like he doesn't recognize them, and his face isn't right. There are too many eyes, and it's all beginning to come apart.

When I come around the corner, he looks up at me and says, out of the blue but clear as day, "What happens when you die, do you think? Your body is empty now, the electrical impulses that once animated it have fled. Is there anything left, when they're gone? Or does a spider crawl inside your mouth, and from there to your brain, slowly spinning its webs among your neurons until, finally, you are something very different?"

So, is that something I saw down there, or is it just a dream? I'll leave that one for you to puzzle out, Dr. Schriver. That seems more your area than mine. What I know is that time didn't seem to pass while Dom and I were underground, though later I would learn that we had been down there for three days.

I know that we ate the candy bars that Dom had brought down—or rather, that I did, Dom said she didn't want any. I know that we saw more of the empty cities, fallen into ruin, and some of the new cities built by the ghouls, round buildings clinging to the ceilings of the caverns in clumps like a spider's egg sac.

Dom never seemed to get tired, but I did. Tired and scared. I wanted to see my mom, wanted to see the sun. I kept thinking about my car, parked there on the street next to the burned out apartment buildings. About my job, my apartment, the jade plant that I hadn't watered that morning, the homework that I hadn't finished for the one college class I was taking online. I told Dom that I wanted to go back up and she smiled sadly and shook her head, but not telling me no, saying, "If you go back up, I don't know if you can come back. At least, not the same way."

And I knew what she meant, just like I know why the guy in my dream is dressed so nicely. But I wasn't ready, I guess, because I told her I wanted to go, and we walked until we found steps that led up. We were holding hands, like when we were little kids, but now Dom was walking a little bit behind me. I started up the steps, and there was light up above me, different than the light that glowed from the rocks and fungi, and Dom's hand was still in mine, but it was heavy, pulling, and then I realized that I was still walking but she had stopped.

I looked back at her, and she was smiling at me, but her face looked different. There was a seam now, running from her bottom lip down along her chin. The place where her face would eventually split open, where mandibles would be. Her eyes were dark and shiny, but she looked happier than I could remember her looking since we were little girls.

"This is where I have to stay," she said, and I knew she was right. I tried to smile back, but I was crying, and I let go of her hand, let her fingertips trickle out of mine one by one, and I turned and went up the steps. That's the last thing I remember before I woke up in a field of milo about a mile from town, covered in a layer of dew, my fingers and toes so cold that I thought I might have already lost them. My clothes, the same ones I had been wearing when I met Dom at the coffee shop three days earlier, were filthy and torn and caked, here and there, with blood that you tell me isn't hers or mine.

I know what you're looking for, what you want me to write here. A story that makes all of this make sense, that turns it into some kind of metaphor. You may not think that I killed Dom, but you *are* pretty sure that she's dead, and you think I know how, why, where. A car accident, with Dom's body in a ditch and a rivulet of blood from her scalp. A fall in some abandoned building, playing that silly game from when we were kids. Something

I feel guilty about, and my guilt is driving me to make up stories. That's what you want. Anything, really, that you can latch on to.

And I wish I could give you that neat if unhappy ending, Mom, Dr. Schriver. I really do. I want you to be okay with this, want you to be happy, so you can see all this as a metaphor if you want to, but you'll have to decide what it represents for yourselves. For me, it's been long enough now, I've talked it through enough times, that I am left with only one thing that I know for sure. There's no door waiting for me in that basement storm shelter anymore. Probably no door waiting for me anyplace else. At least, not the kind that you go through without first paying a toll.

I had my chance, and I got scared, but there's another way down into the Hollow Earth, and I guess I'm just desperate enough for saying Bloody Mary three times in the mirror to be worth the risk, after all. Because if there's anything I regret, it isn't that I left Dom in that place. It's that she got to stay, and I didn't.

VETERAN OF THE FUTURE WARS

The air itself is made of fire. No, not fire. A kind of incandescent, burning light. The aurora borealis brought down to earth, the opalescent sheen of the sun on the scales of my carapace, petroleum spreading over still water. That last one, that is an anachronism, isn't it, because I have never seen petroleum, not in this life, but I can remember it from the world before. There is a word for the light, a series of clicks and buzzings, but it stays lost on the tip of my mandibles.

The light is a weapon. It comes from a creature at once like me and unlike me, one that hunkers down on the ground before us, plates opening up on its hindquarters to display a glowing membrane which fills the air with the burning light. To us it is nothing, a crackle of static against our antennae, but to our enemies, whose eyes and other sensory organs are attuned to a life spent underground, it is disorienting at best, sometimes even deadly.

Ahead of me, the ground churns with them. They come from trap doors in the earth, pouring out of their oubliettes to swarm over the ranks of our troops. Like us, they come in all shapes and sizes, but where our variations are uniform, cultivated, intelligently designed, theirs feel haphazard. A chaos of forms caught halfway between one state and another. Bones held together with sticky webbing, bodies still festooned in tatters of the cloth ornamentation of another time, another world. The same world that I can almost remember...

Where am I? This building with its long, strangely quiet hallways. Its carefully placed potted plants. On the floor there are occasional lines laid down with strips of colored tape, telling someone where to go, where to stop. Telling who? Are they telling me? I sit in a chair, mechanical, wheeled. I feel that I can walk, and yet I don't stand up to make the attempt. People pass me, from time to time, in blue uniforms that I know the word for: scrubs. They hardly give me a second look. How long have I been in this place?

My mother holds my small hand in hers as we walk into the man's tent. I think that we're going to see another revival preacher; Mother has taken me to so many revival preachers, over the years. So many strange little churches in empty storefronts. So many crystals and cards and boards and séances around tables with our hands clasped together in the dark. I remember my mother's brother, the last time I saw him, asking her if there was anything that she *didn't* believe. Sometime, years from now, I will learn the word "theosophist," and I will wonder if that is what my mother was, all along.

Now, though, I am in the man's tent, and my mother is holding my hand, and I know that he isn't like the other revival preachers. The tent is neat and clean inside, and above the opening is a sign with an eye painted in purple and the words "Petrie Warns of the Future to Come!" Inside there are metal chairs, like at some of the revivals, but the ground isn't grass or dirt but scraps of carpet laid down, and on the table along the front of the room are jars filled with sticks and bits of grass and something else inside that moves around.

Mother takes a seat in the second row from the front and I sit down beside her, though I want to move up, look closer at what is in the jars. I lean forward in my seat instead, Mother still holding my hand, her own palm sweaty in mine because it is June and outside I can hear the cicadas.

When the man comes out, it doesn't take me long to realize that he isn't a preacher, he's a prophet. He calls himself Mr. Petrie, and he says that he has seen a vision of what is to come. A true vision, of the race that will replace mankind when there is no place for humans left in this world. He holds up one of the jars and shakes it, and from inside I hear a buzzing sound. "Beetles," he says, and I suddenly recognize the shapes that creep behind the glass.

That night, the dreams begin.

The door seals itself behind me. I have forgotten how far underground we are, though I was told by Mrs. Hammish. Somewhere in the heart of a mountain, a mile above sea level, or what was once sea level, and now maybe a mile underground, for all I know. Like that vault of seeds in Norway, the one that flooded so long ago.

Ahead of us is another door. Not like the heavy, pressurized door that closed behind us, this one is more like a normal door, albeit the normal door of some grand ballroom. There is gilt around the edges, and above the door is a symbol, a scarab, the mark of our Order. Those few of us who found a way to survive.

The deniers denied for far too long, because the other option was too horrible to contemplate. The sea levels rose and rose, and with them came other things. Crawling oozes of human bone and deep-sea slime that encroached further and further onto the land. At first people struck out at them from fear, but later it became clear that they were coming in greater and greater numbers, even as the remaining humans fought amongst themselves over dwindling resources, as the natural creatures of the sea died out, as the oceans ate the land and it grew so hot that just stepping outside during the day was a death sentence in much of the world.

Those who didn't deny turned instead to

science, but if science had ever had a chance of correcting our course, it had waited too long, that's what Mrs. Hammish says. Only a few of us saw the truth—that the age of humanity was over, and it was time for a new age to begin. Only a few of us plumbed the depths of ancient secrets and discovered hermetic rituals that could usher in a new golden age. The true philosopher's stone, capable of transmuting the base metal of finite flesh into the gold of immortality. In the tube that I carry between my gloved hands, the jewel-toned beetle buzzes against its confinement.

In the ballroom beyond the door all the men and women wear tuxedos and ball gowns. This is a fancy occasion, perhaps the greatest occasion in the history of the human race, because it is the last occasion. Outside, the ocean waters are lapping at the doors of our final sanctuary, and with them the strangely bodied invaders from the deep.

I am not dressed in quite the same finery, but I am wearing my nicest clothes. What my grandmother would have called my Sunday best. I don't hold the same rank as Mrs. Hammish, because I was not born into money. I brought expertise to the Order, not wealth, and that makes me less in their eyes, but still, like them, I will be preserved.

We are unclear as to the particulars of how the transformation will occur. Some think that we will be held in a kind of stasis, like insects trapped in amber, until the flood waters recede. Others believe that we will simply preserve our current bodies, albeit in a "perfected state" that will outlast the current climatological calamity. There are some among our number who liken the dying world outside our doors to the great deluge of the Bible, but most of us see such comparisons as simplistic. "We strive for an older knowledge," that's what Mr. Gregson says.

Most of the men and women in the ballroom are much older than I am. Many of them can remember a time from before the world was dying, or, at least, dying so quickly, so obviously. And yet, a part of me can remember that time as well. I remember holding my mother's hand—not the mother who died of cancer in a hospital ward in an already half-abandoned St. Louis that was being eaten by the Mississippi River, a different mother—in a revival tent, hearing a man talk to me about beetles.

That mother was a seeker for truth, and that's what I am, as well, and I think that perhaps I have found it, or at least a part of it, in this room full of people who all wear scarab rings on their fingers, just as I do, just like the one that Boris Karloff wore in *The Mummy*, a movie that I have never seen but can remember with vivid clarity from some other time, some other life. I can hear the voice of Zita Johann, who made hardly any other movies but made a strong impression in that one, saying, "I want to live, even in this strange new world."

They have brought me here because I helped them to find the truth, too. To find some way to survive beyond this life, in some strange new world. But I think that they may be surprised.

We drive them back to their holes in the ground with our superior weapons. I myself can feel the plasma—we have another word for it, but I cannot now call it to mind—building in my auxiliary arms, and I unleash it in a bolt of purple lightning that leaves behind it the vacuum smell of ozone, of burnt air, which I feel in the twitch of my antennae.

I am not a warrior, but in this battle, we are all warriors, and even my kind can generate this energy and unleash it against our foes.

They call themselves ghouls, but we have a number of other names for them, all derogatory. Some of us were aware of them even before the waters began to recede, but shortly afterward we all knew of the threat they posed. They had been waiting for this moment for centuries; biding their time in the shadows beneath graves and caverns, in the hollow places inside the earth, waiting for the time when the surface world died out and they could reclaim it once more. Except that they weren't expecting us.

We had already crushed the things from the sea by the time these *ghouls* emerged from their hidey holes, and though they outnumber us by who-can-say-how-many, we will crush them as well. They can stay in the dark of their dungeons if they so wish, but the surface belongs to us.

A nurse is asking me my name, but I can't remember it. They call it a "memory care facility," this place in which I am imprisoned. Sometimes I can remember that, and other times I can't. I know this. I know there are gaps, times when I cannot remember where I am, or when. They say that's why they keep me here, that it is for my own good that they restrict where I go, what I do. They say that, and perhaps they're right—I've seen the other poor inmates of this place, seen them wander in their attempts to return to some other time, some other place. Would I do the same, if left to my own devices?

It is built to look like a house, for the most part, although it is a house where a great many of us live. We are like children again, each of us with our own bedrooms, and the attendants in their blue scrubs are like our new parents. Days like today, I have given up trying to explain to them what I can barely explain to myself. Have I lost the present? Sometimes, but I have also gained pasts and futures that spin out through the universe without number. I have gained other worlds than these, or all the worlds that this one has been, and may yet be. How can I be expected to occupy them all at once?

Sometimes, they let me sit out in the garden. That's what they call it, but it is really more just a lawn, surrounded with a tall brick fence to keep us all where we belong. There are paths of that soft black stuff they use to make the beds of children's playgrounds—made, they tell me, from ground up tires, bones from the earth, transformed and returning once again to the earth—so that if we fall we do not hurt ourselves.

I stay in my wheelchair, for the most part, and sit where they put me. Sometimes, when no one is looking, I put my foot down and stamp on the ground, trying to see if it is hollow underneath, for I know that *they* are down there, even now.

The paths lead to places where the attendants have stationed flowers arranged in pots, to a fountain hardly bigger than a birdbath so that none of us can drown ourselves in it. I ask them to sit me out in the grass, near a tree whose name I can't remember but which grows white blossoms that attract insects. I sit there and I watch the beetles and I wait for a time when I am a warrior in shining armor.

The first night after my mother took me to see the man in the tent, I wake from a dream and I wake screaming. I am drenched in sweat, and the darkness in my room seems to crawl around me. I scream until my mother is there, until she is holding me in her arms, wincing involuntarily at the clamminess of my skin.

I try to tell her about the dream, but I don't have the words for it anymore. They fled even as the dream images fled, as the reality of my bedroom rushed back in around me. I was fighting things that came up out of the dark. Holes opened in the ground and there were monsters shaped like men but with mouths like spiders. They crawled on their hands.

In the dream I wasn't afraid of them, but I hated them. Awake, I am *very* afraid. I think that there's one in my closet, under my bed. I make my mother check, and, dutifully, she does, but there is nothing but dust and boards. "What's under the boards?" I ask her, and she tells me to just go back to sleep, that it wasn't real.

Wasn't it? I know what's under the boards. There's a space, dark and filled with webs and dust, and there's the foundation of the house and under that dirt…but what's under *that*? I lie in bed, and I look at the walls of my bedroom in the glow from the nightlight, and I try to tell myself that this is what's real, not my dream, but it no longer feels real. It feels like the dream is just on the other side of the walls, ready to push them down.

Outside, June bugs bang themselves against the window screen.

Beyond the ballroom, past another door, is the ritual chamber. "This isn't mysticism," I hear Mr. Gregson mansplaining to some of the other members of our order as we walk in, "that's what I keep trying to tell Kellyanne. It is simply a new type of science, applying a new scientific understanding to secrets that the ancients already knew."

I'm not sure I agree with him, but I also know better than to argue. Especially now, when the culmination is so close at hand. Certainly, the ritual chamber *looks* like mysticism, though I can also see arguments for Mr. Gregson's claims of new-old science. The chamber is enormous, a huge bite taken out of the interior of the mountain. They say that it was once intended to store nuclear waste, or as a kind of last-ditch fallout shelter for the President and his cohorts to fall back to. Whatever it was once intended to be, now it is ours.

The beds wait for us in rows that extend like the spokes of a wheel, and between them run metal tubes that connect, here and there, to incandescent bulbs. Right now they glow a low green, but they will burn brighter once we have lain ourselves down.

Beds isn't right, either. They are slabs. This is a morgue, a tomb. We are going to be mummified, like the Egyptians of old, but we will not be preserving ourselves for some distant afterlife. We are preserving ourselves for tomorrow, transforming our bodies to survive in a world that is, itself, transformed, for, having failed to reach the stars, what other option is available to us?

We lie on the slabs. Mrs. Hammish is nearby, to my left hand side. Her body is so old, her skin so papery and liver-spotted. I wonder why she would cling to this life after spending so much time here.

In the center stands the head of our Order, a man I have never met, though I know his name, of course, we all do. The man whose financing, whose vision helped to begin this quest for a new life in a new world. Would I recognize him if I saw his face? I can't say, for now, as every time I have seen him, his visage is covered by a golden scarab mask.

Hermetic magic. Did you know that bee-tles can bury themselves in times of drought? They essentially die, and are resurrected hun-dreds of years later. That is what we plan to do, in one form or another. The head of our Order holds up a rod that is connected to the tubes and coils that line the floor. The bulbs begin to glow brighter, their color now a rain-bow hue.

We each unscrew the ends of our tubes, the beetles alive in our hands. At his word, we place them in our mouths, feel their many feet scrabble against our tongues, our teeth.

I am just a researcher, a seeker, and I know that I will not be the equal of the men and women who lie down to undergo this meta-morphosis with me. They expect to be born a new golden race, like the ones some of them claim were humanity's forebears in times be-fore recorded history. I don't expect anything of the sort, but I have long since run out of options, and so have they. Would they still be here, if they knew what I know? That's a ques-tion that I cannot answer for them.

In the new world that is to come, I will be a lower caste than these people who have been, throughout this life and the others that I can remember, my social betters, but in spite of that I find myself smiling as I am one of the first to shed my flimsy human skin, my carapace new and shiny and beautiful and iridescent as the pearl inside an oyster.

PANDORA

In the Dreamtime, I am the girl I want to be. Not the girl I would actually be if I went through the transition, took the hormones, went under the knife. That girl would still be tall and fat and gawky—like a pear with toothpicks stuck in to make arms and legs. The girl in the Dreamtime is the girl I long to see when I look in the mirror, the one who can wear all the cute outfits that I run my fingertips lovingly across as I walk through the stores, when I think no one is looking.

My dreams are the only time I can ever be her. Ever feel the body in which I am comfortable; slim and balanced, the hands and feet, fingers and lips and eyes all behaving as I want them to, no longer at odds with the image I have of myself, the poise I wish I could cultivate but never, ever can.

It has taken me years to get the balance right. Most of us don't have a lot of control over our dreams. When we sink below the oceans of sleep and the dark waters close over our heads, all we see are kaleidoscope images taken from our waking life, rearranged, thrown together. Sometimes we drag nightmares up from our subconscious—our fear of pain, of intimacy or its failure, the panic terror that comes with a loss of control—other times we live out our fantasies, but seldom with the lucidity we would prefer.

These dreams, the ones most of us are familiar with, aren't the Dreamtime. They are like a lake, and the Dreamtime a city submerged at its bottom. Most of us can never dive deep enough to get to the place where true dreaming happens, where it comes from, but perhaps every now and then one of us gets a glimpse, and that glimpse pushes us to find a way to dive deeper and deeper, a voice in the back of our minds always warning us that one day we may not be able to come up for air.

For me, it was a particular combination of things. The right sleeping pills, the right bedtime ritual. I had tried melatonin and

candles, incense and one of those noise machines that you can buy at Bed, Bath, & Beyond. I found that music helped more than
soothing sounds, but the music had to be just
right. I first made my way to the Dreamtime
with Juno Reactor's "God is God" on repeat.
Later I had to vary it up in order to keep finding my way down deep enough.

The drugs were the hardest part. Trying different pills, coming up with reasons to tell
the doctor why each one in succession didn't
work. Finally, the pills that did the trick, along
with everything else. Tiny and round, a blue
the color of the night sky in a cartoon. Lately
I've taken to cutting them up, grinding them
down, stretching them out. Mix them in with
a little bit of absinthe and swallow the whole
thing in one gulp. It tastes terrible—the pills
bitter on my tongue, the absinthe like licorice
that has gone bad—but I find that it sinks
me through the night waters faster, down to
where the real Dreamtime lives.

I've wondered before, if other people can see
the Dreamtime like I can. And if so, does it
look the same to them as it does to me? Is
it something that we each find in ourselves,

changed subtly from one person to the next? And yet I know that it isn't a purely subjective place, like the surface dreams to which we are accustomed. I know that there are things here that do not come from within me, from my mind or even some buried part of me, some residual tribal memory. There are things in the Dreamtime that are *true*, things that dwell there and would be there even without me to observe them.

If it is in fact a place at all, the way we normally think of them, I don't know what it is called. I took the name from a book about Australia and Aboriginal culture. It seemed to fit. Those I have met here, if they have a name for this place at all, each seem to have their own. So for me it is the Dreamtime, and that is how it remains.

I am lying in my bed. The night-blue drugs and the absinthe are bitter on my tongue, sweet in the back of my throat, but I'm losing their taste. In the tips of my fingers and my toes there is a tingling that slowly turns to nothing as the body that I have hated for so long drifts away. I can still see my bedroom, still see the textured paint on the wall, still see the popcorn ceiling, but it is leaving me behind. I am sinking into the red bedspread, or perhaps it is flowing into me, and the pillows are growing up around me, becoming mountains.

For a time I can see the music, weaving like smoke or vines through the air, though I can no longer hear it. The television is on, but the sound is muted, so the light is simply a changing flicker, like an old-fashioned projector in the dark. There are drums where the music used to be, and a far-off fluting.

The girl I want to be is standing in front of a door. It's the door to my apartment, from the inside, but it also isn't. It's painted red, and is made of metal, and from the other side of it I can feel a bass thrumming, like the heartbeat of some animal so large that it would make a whale seem like a minnow. The girl I want to be presses her palm to the door—her nails are painted verdigris blue—and the vibration spreads up my arms to my elbows, my shoulders. My heartbeat slows, to match the beat behind the door.

A panel slides open—was it there before?—and someone looks out through yellow eyes with goatlike irises. They ask for a password, and the girl I want to be knows it immediately, though I cannot understand the word that comes falling from my lips, painted to match my nails, the liner around my eyes. The door slides open, and the heartbeat comes pouring out in a wash of neon light, transforming into club music as it does.

On the other side of the door is a dance club, where people move and thrash on a floor made of ancient flagstones. The strange, flat light that seems to leak from everywhere washes their flesh to shades of purple and blue, their bodies scored with tattoos and raised scars and ridges and iridescent scales that are maybe incredible body modifications, maybe natural. I try to follow the music, to focus on it, to commit its rhythms to memory, but I am no longer hearing it with my ears. It is vibrating in my bones, in my heartbeat, in the rush of blood to my labia.

The ceiling of the club is made of the same stone as the floor, the same stone as the columns which support it, carved with snakes and the faces of skulls worn into grim caricature by countless eons of geologic time. In the corners crouch statues that could be sphinxes or hounds, spiders or serpents, and I have no idea how it is that I cannot tell the one from the other. Through the grooves in the stone, where blood may once have run and may yet run again, narrow tubes carry neon and argon that change in color with the rhythm of the music that I can no longer hear because it is inside me now, pushing me forward, carrying me along the edges of the dance floor, to where another door waits beneath an arch of stone.

The door here is cushioned, and I know that it leads to the club's back room, just as I know that isn't what I will find on the other side when the door folds open.

Beyond the red padded door stone steps lead down, down, down into a darkness lit by more tubes of neon that trace along the ceiling of a natural cave, throwing the shadows of the stalactites long and dark. Liquid drips onto the steps, and each drop leaves behind a luminous gleam, like the light of some deep sea creature, or a pale lightning bug glowing and fading.

At the bottom of the steps, the corridor opens up into a vast plateau. Its roof looks like the night sky, but I know that it isn't. The stars here are painted on, asterisks of some luminous chalk that glitters weakly far above. The moon crawling slowly up that wall is a fungus, a puffball that gives off a shifting fox-fire glow, now blue, now green as it creeps along.

On the plain are the ruins of cities, cut from the same stone as the nightclub, showing architectural influences from a variety of eras and locales. In the distance, rugose domes like those at Angkor Wat show rents and clefts in their roofs, while closer on strange tombs tower up from the flat plateau, with sarcophagi set into their sides, the figures not those of living faces but careful sculptures of giant bodies eaten away by death. Each one must be twelve feet tall or more.

Across this plateau two armies clash. On one side, what looks at a glance like men in suits of lacquered armor. On the other, dark shapes that scuttle and scurry, wearing the rags of suits and shrouds. As the girl I want to be walks closer, I can see that the armored men are beetles, varying in size from broad-shouldered humanoids to enormous giants that plow forward on four of their six legs to tiny creatures no larger than a dog, scuttling among their superiors. Some walk erect, as men do, their middle limbs small and folded close to their bodies, carrying balls of writhing purple energy that reminds me, morbidly, of a bug zapper. From time to time they hurl the balls into bolts of thick purple lightning which leave behind an afterimage in the air.

The other things look less human at first, but more and more as I draw closer. Their heads are like spiders, like frogs, topped with only the very wisps of white hair, filled up with too many eyes, their jaws splitting open into multi-part mouths. Some have limbs that are chitinous and end in sharp barbs; these scuttle on all fours. Other still walk as men, their hands simply twisted into arthritic claws, their faces still retaining some semblance of their lost humanity. Lost, indeed, for they are marked as having been human once by the vestiges of their clothes—funeral finery, the suits and ties, the black dresses and, among the older of their number, the sackcloth and winding sheets in which they were laid into the ground.

They are less organized than the beetles, more savage, but they make up in numbers what they lack in finesse or weaponry. They pour up from holes in the ground that then swing shut behind them like trap doors, and from time to time I see, moving among their number, larger things, still spider-like in shape but seemingly made up of wrong angles and bones and tendons of cobweb. What they are I cannot say, but that they will grind any beetle they encounter to dust and jewel-toned grit I have no doubt. Spiders eat bugs, after all.

"When do dreams happen?" I asked my doctor once.

"When you're asleep," he answered, over his shoulder.

"That's not what I mean," I said. "I mean that sometimes, when you dream, you're a little kid. The way you were twenty years ago, or ten. Other times you're someone who doesn't exist at all, at least not yet. Maybe someone you were before you were born, or someone you'll be after you die, or no one who will ever be anything at all. So when you're in a dream, *when* are you? Are you in the past, the present, or the future?"

He sat down on the little rolling stool and looked at me. "You know that's not really my field?" he asked, and I nodded. Then he paused, seeming to really consider my question, which I appreciated more than he probably knew. "Then I guess I'd say they take place in all of them, or none of them. Past, present, and future in one. Some time that's outside of time, and also in all of the places time will ever be."

The spiders and the beetles ignore the girl I want to be, knowing, somehow, that she is not a part of their war. As I walk amongst them, along the edges of the battle, I wonder when this battle is happening, and if maybe I'm not actually where they are at the same time as them. Could I walk right through one, would either of us even know? Is this what a ghost is? A person in another time, maybe in a dream, walking through the place that you will be walking through in a hundred years, or that they will be walking through a hundred years from now?

On the other side of the wide plateau, archways lead down into the depths beneath the domed buildings. The walls here are carved with bas-reliefs, their shapes outlined in neon and argon. They seem to be battling, and when I turn my head the designs seem to shift. Humans, their features square, are outlined in tubes of yellow. They throw down giant monsters into an enormous prison, like a honeycomb or the surface of the moon. I can't make out the monsters very well, the neon lights that once illuminated them have all burned out.

The yellow neon shows cities like the one I passed through the ruins of above, where saurian shapes—these are green—seem to live and work alongside the golden people, and from their comparative scale I can tell that these men are giants. Perhaps it is their tombs I witnessed on the plain outside. But other forces infiltrate the golden cities, represented by tubes of argon blue that flicker, painting their carvings in a fitful illumination. Here are the spiders, great crouching things that go into the golden people or come out of them, it's difficult to say.

As I watch the carvings, the girl I want to be is walking deeper and deeper into the tunnel. It is square, not a natural cave like the one leading down from the club, and carvings adorn every inch of its surface. Purple lights mark shapes rising up out of the sea, at once bulbous and strangely familiar, and from time to time the lights are bright enough that I can make out the carving of a human skull in their bulk. Then other lights, in all colors, seem to flood back in, as beetle shapes, like Egyptian carvings of scarabs, seem to fall downward from the sky, driving back the purple-lit carvings from the sea, and even the electric blue carvings of the spiders.

At the end of the tunnel is not a door but a chamber, easily as large as the one containing the plateau where I had witnessed the battle above. Here is another city, the architecture of similar style, but it has fallen much farther into ruin. Almost none of the roofs remain intact at all. Tombs lie broken open, scattering jewels and other, unfamiliar riches. Some of the tombs are enormous, obviously meant to harbor the body of something even larger than the giants I had seen in the carvings.

The girl I want to be walks through the streets of the dead city, but with every step she takes, I know that it isn't dead, not entirely. Finally her eyes leave the ruined walls around her and climb the domed sides of the enormous natural cavern. Up the walls run thick strands of webbing, anchoring round dwellings like the egg sacs of arachnids to the ceiling of the cavern, and from them come and go the relatives of the spider-like creatures that swarm the plain of battle above.

All around the girl I want to be I can now hear their scuttling motion, just around the next corner, just on the next street of the city's picked-over skeleton. My heart thuds in her chest, my breath catches in her throat, but her steps continue unerringly, and eventually I see our destination, a great congeries of domes, nearly all fallen in. At one time they must have been a palace or temple that would dwarf the most massive structures of the waking world, and as the girl I want to be walks up their steps, festooned with mosaic tiles whose meanings have long since been lost to dust, I see that the entire building is now draped in a blizzard of cobwebs, like a Halloween haunted house.

The doors, however, stand open, and the girl I want to be passes through them and on the other side I find more stairs leading down, a spiral this time, a massive corkscrew burrowing deeper and deeper into the earth of dreams. On every side of it darkness stretches forever, but neon lights line the steps, and glowing moss fills in the cracks in the ancient stone. I walk down it for far too long, until it seems to be turning around me while I stand still. If I were awake, my feet would feel like they were driven full of nails, my calves would be burning, but in the Dreamtime, each step still feels like the first.

At the bottom of the spiral stairs there is another doorway, this one hexagonal, like the chambers of a beehive. The light on the other side is blue, but also like a black light. It changes the colors of my clothes, my nails. Washes my skin a strange blue of its own.

Beyond the doorway a throne room waits. The throne sits atop a stepped pyramid that rises up and up, and all along its sides scuttle the spider-like creatures, and suddenly I know their names. They are ghouls, and the woman who sits upon the throne at the top of the pyramid is their queen, though it has not always been so.

The girl I want to be walks up the steps of the pyramid, and at first the ghouls make as if to threaten her, darting forward for a moment before skulking back. I wonder why, and as I look around I see that the girl I want to be is flanked by great cats, shadows that have stepped out of the deeper shadows here at the bottom of the world, their eyes a green like glowing jade. They keep the ghouls at bay until I reach the foot of the throne.

The Ghoul Queen does not look like her subjects. Her skin is pale and shines with a porcelain whiteness that a romance author would describe as alabaster. The clothes she wears I cannot make sense of—an impression of gauzy drapes that seem to move in a breeze that does not exist—but her face and hands are covered in gold. She wears a golden mask with jeweled eyes and fangs like the stylized face of a spider, and her fingers are encased in long golden claws, sheathes that run all the way up her forearms to her elbows.

Her throne is part of a statue that looks like it might once have been human, or human-oid, but like her has changed over time. It has no legs but many arms, all of them jointed wrongly, and it is edged in neon tubing that produces the strange blue/black light. The statue's features are difficult to read, but in the center of its chest is another neon light, this one in the shape of a heart—not a Valentine's Day heart, but an actual human heart—but the neon has burned out. No, more than burned out, burned into something that is the opposite of light. A black hole that seems to pierce through the statue and into some deeper darkness far beyond the bounds of the Dreamtime or this inner earth. A darkness deeper than the deepest space.

The Ghoul Queen smiles behind her mask, though I don't know how I know, and she says, "So you're here. I didn't know when it would be."

The girl I want to be opens her painted lips to speak, but I don't know what to say, and I guess neither does she.

"Has it been a thousand years, or has it been a day, since I was a little girl at my Nana's knee?" the Ghoul Queen asks, then shakes her head, a gesture so minor, so small, that I should not be able to see it. She is looking away from me now. To my left. Not at the cat-shapes which still prowl beside me, but at something far away. "The war will never end," she says, "and even if it does, there will always be another. We are all of us struggling from our cocoons, but on the other side there is only ever another cocoon."

The ghouls seem to bunch around her. These closest to her are, most of them, the farthest from the shapes they once had when they were living people, and yet there is one who stands near her, in her shadow, who still seems to almost be a man. His hands are blackened, but have not begun to twist. He keeps his face turned away, yet I can see the gleam of too many eyes.

"I brought to this place what I could—we all do, I suppose—but this is not the way it is meant to be." The Ghoul Queen's voice is wistful. "Someone said it to me once, long ago or maybe yesterday. Nothing lasts forever, not even forever."

The ghoul in her shadow breaks away from the others, and I know somehow that I am supposed to follow him. He leads me around her throne, and as I pass by the side of her I can see the slump of her shoulders and I know that she is so very tired.

On the other side of her throne is a door, much smaller than the others I have passed through, and I have to duck my head. I think of *Alice in Wonderland* as the ghoul holds the door to the small portal open for me, and shuts it behind.

This door is made of wood, and the place I enter smells like a crawlspace. It is dark here, the neon lights that have lit my way through the underworld are gone, and I feel my way forward with my fingertips against rough-hewn walls coated in dust. The cat shadows have been left behind on the other side of the wooden door, save for one tiny kitten who stays at my side, threading between my legs as I take tentative steps forward, her eyes the only embers of light.

Beyond the door are more stairs leading down, the steps narrow, the passage narrow, only large enough for the girl I want to be to pass. My waking body would have to contort absurdly, if it could squeeze through at all. The steps lead down and down, making sharp and sudden turns as my palms slap against the wall ahead of me. I know that I am descending down beneath the pyramid on which the Ghoul Queen's throne stands. I know that I am descending down below the bottom of the world. What is lower than that, I wonder?

At the bottom is another wooden door. It feels familiar, like the door of the shed in my backyard when I was little. I push it open, and step out of the trunk of a tree. The tree is petrified, the roots and branches all turned to stone, to polished ash. Petrified too is the creature that twines at the base of the tree, like a serpent with small, malformed hands. Its teeth are sunk into the root, and there it rests forever.

The door in the trunk faces across a chamber that is incredibly tall but not wide. It cannot be here, and I know it, even in the Dreamtime. Its roof would rise far above the Ghoul Queen's throne. Yet here it is. On the other side of the chamber is another hexagonal door. Like the heart in the Ghoul Queen's statue it seems to suck in everything around it, yet this is not a simple absence of light, it is a substance. The collapsing heart of a black hole star given mineral shape. In the black diamond, I can see my own reflection refracted. There is the girl I want to be, behind and beside her the girl I *would* be if I had the surgeries and treatments, beyond that the body that is even now sleeping in my bed, the child I once was, and, stretching out behind us, hundreds of other images. The people I have been, may yet be, will never become.

I reach up and put my hand against the door and it shimmers. A ripple passes through it, and then the black glass forgets to be glass and becomes liquid that spills around my feet, only to then forget to be liquid and be nothing at all, the stone floor as dry as it ever was. Now, however, the doorway stands open.

From the other side come giants. Monsters. I recognize them, in a way, from the carvings in the tunnel above, the ones who fought against the golden people but whose lights had all burned out. The first past the threshold is like a piece of the night that has broken loose and fluttered down, walking upon its wings in the dark. Once it was worshipped as a god in the world above, and when I close my eyes I can see its altars. Now its six blind eyes burn red in the cavern, and its breath smells of mummies and cenotes and old, old death. It moves past me with a brush of fur and leather.

Behind it comes a thing that is all bulk, dragged forward through the doorway by legs and arms that end in tiny points or hooks, its haunches brushing the sides of the opening, tentacles that depend from either side of its head quivering in the air before it like antennae. Its face glows with a pink light that shines from within its multi-part mouth, from behind its eyes.

As the titans leave their prison behind, they disappear up the walls of the chamber, and

I know that they will emerge somewhere far above. In the world where the beetles fight their battles against their foes, in the ruined cities of the ghouls themselves, in the age of the golden race, in the waking world that I left behind. The Dreamtime is all time and no time, and these creatures have returned to restore a balance that was lost somewhere along the way. The first was like a bat, after all, and bats eat beetles *and* spiders.

On and on they come, a thing like a snail that shines with the light of a deep-sea fish, a creature that moves on countless segmented legs and waves claws like an enormous crab, until dozens have left their prison and all that remains is the doorway and the humming darkness beyond. Yet I can feel that there is one more who still lurks on the other side of the door. She has a name, it lies on the tip of my tongue, yet it is older than memory. I can hear her there, breathing in the dark, but she does not drag her way forward, so I go in to find her.

I wake with a start, back in my other body, the one that is heavy with maleness and fat that I know I should shed but never do because, deep down, I know it won't help. The body whose bones are still too long, too heavy. Wrong shaped, and the inside of me aching to crawl out as those beasts did from that deep hole, but knowing that even on the outside, things would never be right. What did the Ghoul Queen say? "On the other side of our cocoon there is only ever another cocoon."

I rise and go to the mirror, pressing my fingertips against the cold glass. I listen for breath, for the tread of some far-off giant. Sometimes, if I stare long enough into my own eyes, I can catch a glimpse of the girl from the Dreamtime, waiting for me there on the other side, but now I see only darkness. I wonder if she will still be there when I go to sleep again, or if she is gone forever. A sacrifice is needed to break ancient bonds and waken great beasts. I weep in the shower as the hot water scalds me, even as I make myself a promise that I will go out tomorrow and buy nail polish and lipstick and eyeliner, though I know it will never be the same, never be enough. Outside, a neon sign buzzes against the night.

Author's Notes

As much as anything else about my writing, my short story collections are known for the author's notes that always accompany each tale. That was something I didn't want to abandon here but, because of the unique way that these stories bleed into one another, I also didn't want the notes to break up the flow of the stories as they usually do. Hence, for this volume, I've kept the notes to the ending, though I trust that longtime readers will find all the inspirations and "behind the scenes" secrets that they're accustomed to here...

"The Insectivore"

At the time I wrote this story for Ross Lockhart's *Cthulhu Fhtagn!* anthology, I had no idea that it was ever going to connect up with

anything else. I was simply looking for something different to do in a Lovecraft vein, and
snagged myself on that line about the race of
beetles replacing humans. From there, I got
the idea of an old man who saw the future
and couldn't think of a way to prevent it from
coming to pass, an element that wouldn't feel
out of place in some of the old noir movies
that I love.

It wasn't until some time later that I wrote
the other stories that would eventually make
up this linked cycle and, in so doing, realized
the importance that these beetles from the future would play in my Hollow Earth mythology and that, therefore, "The Insectivore" had
been a part of it all along.

"New, and Strangely Bodied"

While "New, and Strangely Bodied" was written after I had already penned several of the
other stories in this book, it is like "The Insectivore" in that I wasn't aware that it was
part of this cycle until after I had finished
and it is, in many ways, the most loosely connected of the bunch.

"New, and Strangely Bodied" borrows its

title from the 1965 film *Die, Monster, Die!*, which is still my favorite Lovecraft adaptation. It borrows its monsters, albeit unconsciously, from *Horror at Party Beach*, of all places. It borrows some of its visuals from Mike Mignola comics. And it borrows its setting from my many trips to the Pacific Northwest over the years, often to attend the H. P. Lovecraft Film Festival.

It was written as an original for Pseudopod, where it was published as part of their 2017 Kickstarter, in an anthology called *For Mortal Things Unsung*. The theme, I was told, was "a thread of Pacific Ocean resonance," and this was the result. "New, and Strangely Bodied" was later reprinted in *Spoon Knife 5* in 2021.

I particularly love the Cargo Cult Video store, and hope that I'll get to revisit it someday.

"No Exit"

The first of the stories written for those three anthology invites I mentioned in my preamble, "No Exit" is also the first story in this volume to deal directly with the Hollow Earth, and it introduces as monsters the creatures that I refer to in my own mind (and sometimes in later stories) as "ghouls," who are the Hollow Earth's "current" inhabitants.

"No Exit" was written for *Lost Highways*, an anthology of road stories edited by D. Alexander Ward and published by Crystal Lake in 2018. I was extremely honored when it was subsequently chosen for inclusion in Ellen Datlow's *Best Horror of the Year*, and then reprinted at *Nightmare Magazine* in 2020, making it one of my most popular and successful stories.

The idea for the narrative itself came about after a long drive that I had taken along the route described in the story. There is a rest stop along the way that boasts unique geography, similar to the one in the tale, albeit not exactly the same. This rest stop has always arrested my attention, and seemed a logical location for a road story—even if it means I may never drive past the place quite the same way again.

"Leandra's Story"

Though this was the last of these tales that I *finished* writing, it was one of the first that

I *began*. From the minute I knew that I was putting together a linked collection of short stories, this was always intended to be the centerpiece of it—a novelette original to this collection that would feature the closest thing the book has to a single main character.

Yet, as you can see, it is not located at the *end* of the book, acting instead as a center in more ways than one, occupying the space in the overarching narrative where the Hollow Earth has begun to open out, gradually introducing more of the mythology that I have built. Here, we have elements of real-life Hollow Earth theorists and churches, alongside many of the other preoccupations that went into the creation of this book.

There are several reasons why Scott Candish is (or was) a stage magician. One of them is undoubtedly Clive Barker's "The Last Illusion," a story that had a profound impact on me and which informed the personalities of some of this story's characters and their relationships. Another is because of the 2006 film *The Prestige*, about dueling stage magicians, which provides one of the two epigraphs which introduce this book.

From the time I started writing most of

these stories, I knew how this one was going to begin, and how it was going to end. This has always been Leandra's story.

"Hollow Earths"

I knew when I accepted an invitation to contribute something for Scott Jones's anthology *Cthonic*, composed of subterranean stories, that I would be able to make some bolder narrative choices in this tale than in some of the others. When putting this collection together, I placed it after "Leandra's Story" because I think it expands the Hollow Earth in ways that make more sense after that tale than before, though it was written, like every other story here, to be able to be read on its own.

More Hollow Earth jargon went into this story than any other, and it samples from just about every iteration of the phenomenon throughout history and literature. There's something about being able to open a door and have what's on the other side not be what should be there that harkens back to Barker again, and has always been something I aspire to in a lot of my writing.

For the line of reasoning about Bloody

Mary, I am indebted to Joey Comeau, and a review he once wrote of the movie *The Innkeepers*. "There's something really satisfying about that desire to terrorize yourself," Comeau wrote, "because it also feels like it will be worth it if those bloody fingers come through the mirror and wrap around your throat. The world will be so much more magical and interesting, and so you kind of hope that it does work."

To the extent that I have ever had a mission statement, that might be it.

"Veteran of the Future Wars"

The last of the three stories written for anthology invitations that kicked off this whole story cycle, this was also the last one to be published, and the one that has maybe the least to do with the Hollow Earth, though it harkens directly back to those beetle people from "The Insectivore."

While the call came all the way back in 2017, this story didn't see publication in *Tales from Arkham Sanitarium* until 2022, by which time every other story in this volume (besides "Leandra's Story" but including

"Pandora") had already been published.

The title is a riff on the Blue Oyster Cult song "Veteran of the Psychic Wars," which was itself co-written by none other than Michael Moorcock.

"Pandora"

If "Leandra's Story" was always going to be the centerpiece of this collection, then "Pandora" was always going to be the story that ended it, wrapped it all up. Written after any of the others, in response to a call from Cody Goodfellow and the late Joe Pulver to contribute a story to *New Maps of Dreams*, a deluxe anthology exploring Lovecraft's Dreamlands, "Pandora" gave me an opportunity to explore the metaphysical space of my Hollow Earth in a way that hadn't been possible in any of the other stories here, while also allowing me to pull together threads from all of them.

It's also one of the most personal stories I've ever written, and I'm very happy to have it close out this very weird collection.

ABOUT THE AUTHOR

Orrin Grey is a skeleton who likes monsters, as well as a Rondo Award-nominated writer, editor, and amateur film scholar who was born on the night before Halloween. You can find him online at orringrey.com.